TIDES

Tracy L. McCutcheon

PublishAmerica
Baltimore

© 2010 by Tracy L. McCutcheon.
All rights reserved. No part of this book may be reproduced, stored in a retrieval system or transmitted in any form or by any means without the prior written permission of the publishers, except by a reviewer who may quote brief passages in a review to be printed in a newspaper, magazine or journal.

First printing

All characters in this book are fictitious, and any resemblance to real persons, living or dead, is coincidental.

PublishAmerica has allowed this work to remain exactly as the author intended, verbatim, without editorial input.

Hardcover 978-1-4512-3543-2
Softcover 978-1-4512-3544-9
PAperback 978-1-4512-6874-4
PUBLISHED BY PUBLISHAMERICA, LLLP
www.publishamerica.com
Baltimore

Printed in the United States of America

For our natural world around us; don't lose hope, we will see you.

Thank you to Brad, Malcolm, Kailey and Paisley, your support and love made this possible.

Table of Contents

CHAPTER 1: THE END 11
CHAPTER 2: NEW SKIN 13
CHAPTER 3: SECRETS REVEALED 24
CHAPTER 4: THE TALK 32
CHAPTER 5: INTRODUCTION 36
CHAPTER 6: FRIDAY NIGHT 43
CHAPTER 7: DEEPEST OCEAN 55
CHAPTER 8: EXPOSED 69
CHAPTER 9: JEALOUSY 77
CHAPTER 10: COMPETITION 84
CHAPTER 11: RESISTING DESIRES 93
CHAPTER 12: BONDS 117
CHAPTER 13: STRUGGLES 122
CHAPTER 14: THE CALM 129
CHAPTER 15: THE TEAM 144
CHAPTER 16: WHAT'S NORMAL? 179
CHAPTER 17: APPLE PIE WITH A SIDE OF MEMORIES 192
CHAPTER 18: REJECTED 201
CHAPTER 19: RALLY THE TEAM 204
CHAPTER 20: THE WAIT 213
CHAPTER 21: MEETING 218
CHAPTER 22: HOPING FOR A SWIM 232

CHAPTER 1

The End

"She's DIEING…I said SHE'S DIEING, if we don't **Try** to forge some kind of union now, we will lose her, and the rest of us won't be far behind!" A short dark haired woman rose to her feet slamming her fist on the table, hoping it would create more impact to her words as she spoke. "I know all of you can see it as well as I can. I plead with you all now…Whose support can I count on?" The little woman reached for the arms of her chair and plunked herself back down on the rose coloured cushion. Now seated at a large round table, she cleared her throat and peered at the others seated around it.

"We have never been ones to interfere or alter the course of destiny. However …" the man to the woman's right got to his feet and looked despondently into the faces of those around the table. "I have never seen it look so bleak. There have always been alternatives. However this time I am much more fearful of the outcome. Perhaps you are right. Perhaps we do need to show them a way to reverse the course they are on and help them to plot a new one. One in which we can all survive." The man stood looking very thoughtful for a moment and as though a new resolve took life in his mind, a look of hope seemed to come over his face. "Yes, I see it now…this is the course we must set. However, the five of us will be here to advise or assist when needed. It is not our course to plot or interfere with." The man looked at the others around the table; each person nodded their heads in agreement. Once he had the approval from the others at the table, he turned his gaze back to the woman. "Let us know when you are ready to proceed, and our eyes and ears will be here for you. We wish this matter a joyful outcome. Be well, my friend of many years." The man gave the woman a nod and a smile, and with that the woman gave her thanks to all, and quickly took her leave. She knew she had much to prepare for the upcoming task, and would need every minute she possessed. Though time was against her, she knew she was ready to run the race, and should she fail, then it would not be for a lack of trying.

CHAPTER 2

New Skin

    The sunlight broke over the horizon; the waters were calm and so was I. It seemed I had only just sat down, and already the events of the day were looming. With the break of the new day I felt a flutter of nerves from somewhere deep within my body. I knew what this day was to hold for me.

    I knew the sand had also been waiting the return of the sun to warm each grain as it had done the day before, for this is what mother had always told me. The sand enjoyed being warmed by the sun, but also liked the shade that the cool evenings offered. I sat on the sand burrowing my feet into its coolness. With one hand I would scoop up a handful of sand, allowing the grains to escape through my fingers. Placing my other hand below, I would enjoy the feel of the grains rushing past my open hand to reunite with the sand around my feet. Such a simple thing, but relaxing in its own way. How I longed to remain in my over-sized sand box away from the rest of the world, but I knew I couldn't hide from what lay ahead. No, it was time to start this day and deal with all it had to offer.

    Brushing the sand from my clothes I stood and turned to walk back to the small shabby cottage near the water. I could feel the sand under my feet. Still such an unfamiliar feeling to me; I knew that it would take some time to get used to it. So many things unfamiliar to me right now; I've been feeling quite overwhelmed by all the recent changes. My sisters and mother had adapted much better than I. Perhaps, in time I too would become more comfortable in my *new skin*. Time—I've had lots of that, but how much more would I have? It was this question that had brought me to this shore in the first place, and only time would tell if things would work out in my favor.

The door to the cottage was slightly ajar and I couldn't remember if I had left it like that, or if Aella had opened the door to see where I had gotten too.

Aella was closest to me, of my two sisters. She and I had spent so much time together that things were unnaturally quiet when she was not near me. She had the ability to calm me when nothing else could. Aella could also stir me up, but I didn't mind so much 'cause, what would life be if it were always calm. I love my sister; she is an important part of my life. Aella was tall and slender with beautiful long light brown hair that spiraled into loose ringlets. Her skin was fair with naturally pink lips. However it was her eyes that held one's attention to her face. So much depth in such a young face; I wondered in the recent weeks if that on its own would be enough to give us away. Mother assured me that it would take more than that for people to catch on. I took comfort in her assurance. Mother could comfort me as well, but not like Aella.

My other sister goes by the name of Serafina. However, she informed us that we were it call her "Fina"; she felt it was more "with the times", she said. She was very confident, and had an air of vanity that she wore like the exclamation mark at the end of a very convincing argument. With her long slim legs and delicate frame you would swear she was a ballerina. She always walked with her shoulders back, and as if Grace should be her middle name. Fina's hair was a brilliant red and she always made efforts to style it with the trendiest looks. Fina could be quite explosive at times. I had overheard people in the town talk about my sister as a 'fiery

Redhead' but I knew it was her temper that made the hair red, not the red hair making the temper.

Beside Fina, I looked quite dowdy. I was the *average* duckling. I lacked their levels of confidence as well. Not as tall as my two sisters in stature, I was much more comfortable away from people where I didn't need to speak or be heard. The most striking thing about me were my eyes; they are as blue as the waters of the tropics. I must say I do love them for that. It's like my own piece of ocean wherever I go. My hair was a sandy blonde colour; it came just below my shoulders with a slight wave throughout, and I suppose it was pretty in its own way.

It was just last week that my mother had gotten the three of us jobs at the local beach club here in Lunenburg. The beach club was small in comparison to the larger club a mile down the beach, however, it was larger than anything I thought I was ready for. Fifty employees seemed so intimidating at this point. I kept questioning in my head, "What if I made a mistake, what if I have forgotten some of Mothers teachings; was it really so important that we "integrate". Well I was certain that Mother thought it was important, so I decided I must try. After all, so much relied upon it.

Our cottage was very tiny in comparison to most of the houses in Lunenburg that I had seen on our walks through town. However, the cottage was just right for our needs. The entrance to the cottage was a single navy blue door that opened into a very modest kitchen. In the centre of the right hand wall was a large fireplace. Made of brick, the fireplace was probably the most eye-catching thing about the cottage's interior. A beautiful old knotted maple mantel was built into the bricks around the fireplace. With such detail and charm, the fireplace didn't have to be lit for the focal point of the room to radiate warmth throughout. To the left of the kitchen was a small washroom, just big enough for its three fixtures, and no more. To the rear of the cottage was a sitting area where a couch and chair sat angled towards the fireplace. The only walls were the ones around the bathroom; the rest of the cottage was wide open, with the large old hardwood plank flooring running its length. In the back left hand corner of the cottage was an old iron spiral staircase that wound its way up to the second level. I suppose you could say the upstairs was modest too. However, it too had a charm of its own. In the back right hand corner was a closet for the 4 of us to share, though we were accustomed to sharing each other's clothes. For the most part, they were pretty humble digs. Mother's bed ran the length of the room, while our beds ran across it, leaving just enough for a walkway between them. I loved this next part of the room: the head of each of our three beds overlooked the fireplace chimney and half of the kitchen below. The beds were pushed up against a 4-foot cast iron spindle railing that ran from the closet in the back to the front wall of the cottage. This railing allowed you to see right through to everything downstairs. My bed was pushed up against the front wall right underneath the window, facing the ocean. It was nice to be so open and to be able to enjoy the sounds from outside.

As I entered our cottage I could smell something different, not bad, just weird. Our cottage didn't usually smell like much of anything, I guess, because we were so close to the ocean and that was such a comforting smell. This new intruding odor just caught me off guard. It was like roses of some sort, but I was unable to locate any flowers that had brought their scent to our little cottage. A moment or two had passed then I realized that Fina was spraying this rose scent from a small bottle Mother had bought yesterday in town. "Come here Naida, let me spray some on you." Fina said.

"Why would I want to smell like something I am not?" I questioned, screwing up my nose. "Please stop spraying that stuff".

"Girls, you must hurry and get ready! Your walk to work will take you at least 10 minutes, so you don't have time to stand here and argue about perfume." Mother glared at the two of us for a moment and then continued making our lunches. Aella was sitting at the back of the cottage dressed and ready to go. She flashed a warm smile at me as I reached for the railing of the staircase. I went up the stairs to our closet to pull out the clothes that everyone agreed would be best for me to wear. Laying the clothes on my bed, I pulled off my sweat top and shorts, and put on a pair of dark blue pants and a white blouse. Mother had told us we would receive uniforms today, but that we needed to look nice when we first arrived at the club. It was early summer, so I decided the sweater wouldn't be necessary.

"Okay girls, your lunches are ready." Mother's voice seemed to sing out to the three of us from downstairs. Mother had told the beach club that we were triplets and very shy, so the Human Resource Manager, Mrs. Snorff said she would do her best to get the three of us in the same department of the Club. This suited me fine because I knew I would need their help if I was going to pull this off. I was terrified, and in addition, I was so conscious of the pull the ocean had on me today. I hurried downstairs to join my sisters. As we left the little cottage I glanced out at the ocean but for only a moment. I knew what I would see but my eyes confirmed what my body was feeling. The calm waters from earlier were now churning as though they were uneasy about something. I hurried along beside my sisters, not tempting a second glance at the water. How would I last the day? I heard Mother's voice call after us, "Aella, please keep watch on your sisters". We stopped and looked at her as she continued. "Help Naida, she is still adjusting" as she threw a glance at the ocean.

"Yes Mother, don't worry. She will be fine with Fina and I." Mother graced us with a warm smile and closed the door to the cottage.

The walk wasn't too bad. It gave me time to try to slow my breathing down enough so my head would stop spinning. However, that lasted only a short time.

Standing at the foot of the wide entrance to the club, Aella put her arm around my shoulder and whispered, "You're going to be fine. Just stay close so we don't get split up". A tiny smile broke over my lips as I nodded at her. The three of us walked up a couple steps to two heavy wooden doors, beautifully detailed with fine carvings. Fina pulled one of the doors open to reveal one of the most striking reception areas I had ever seen—*not that I have seen many*. The entrance appeared to be done all in marble, glass, with wood accents. To the left of the entrance was a long marble desk where two very pleasant looking women stood. Both of the women wore matching blue blazers with white blouses underneath. Pinned over the left breast pocket appeared to be a golden plaque inscribed with their names. The women looked very similar to one another, but neat and happy to help all the same. To the right of the entrance was a glass shelving unit. Just beyond, there were several very comfortable looking chairs. Most of the walls were made of glass except for the one straight ahead adjacent to a short flight of stairs. This wall had the most amazing waterfall built into it. The water cascaded over a copper-like backing into a huge stone basin that was also built into the wall at floor level. Right dead centre of the entrance was a low circular table with a large vase containing a beautiful fresh floral arrangement. It wasn't until I felt a tug on my arm that I realized my sisters hadn't stopped to take in the beauty of the room like I had. I guess I had been standing there staring at everything when Aella noticed I wasn't beside her anymore, and come back for me.

There was an orientation for all the new summer employees this morning. With a second gaze around the sleek marble entrance, I could see several other people our age milling about, off to the right, near the chairs where a large sign read **New Staff Orientation and Training, Please Wait Here**. Aella and I walked over to join Fina and the group that was forming, apparently waiting for the same thing. There were about 10 of us in total, some looking a little nervous. We weren't waiting very long before a large woman with black-rimmed glasses and very puffy, unnaturally black hair joined the group. She wore a blue blazer (like the ones the women at the desk were wearing), with a matching knee-length skirt. The outfit likely fit her at one time, however, she looked rather like a stuffed sausage today. "Good Morning everyone," she started with a kind voice that seemed quite forced, as though her vocal chores weren't used to being in such a tone. "Thank you for coming. My name is Mrs.

Snorff, however, most of you already know that, as we have already met once or twice." Clearing her throat, she continued, "I will take you on a tour of our facility and then divide you up into your groups for your training. Please stay close; I don't want anyone getting lost on the first day." She smiled directly at me. Could she see how nervous I was? Staying close would not be an issue. Aella stayed right by my side. Fina was starting to mingle her way through the group flashing smile after smile at most of the boys as she maneuvered to the other side of the group. She glanced back at us. With a wink of her eye at us, we both knew she was already *integrating*.

The tour was hurried through the reception area. Mrs. Snorff made note of the girls standing at the desk, and a few other attributes of the room, but got us on our way rather quickly. I had only ever seen the Beach Club from outside at a very *different* angle. This was *far* more beautiful than I expected. Leaving the main entrance, we walked up the wide marble staircase beside the waterfall. At the top we entered a huge lounge, with a high ceiling. The opposite wall from where we stood was all windows facing the warm, inviting beach and *ocean*. It was stunning; with small circular tables and lounge chairs in front of the windows. A few guests sat evaluating at the new help for the summer. To the left of where we stood was a long oak bar, with a row of barstools set along the front of it. Just beyond the bar was a stone fireplace with a couple wingback chairs facing it. This room was amazing. But Mrs. Snorff was on a mission to get us through the tour and into our groups as soon as possible, so we didn't stop to linger. We were herded into a hallway to the right of the lounge. Mrs. Snorff pointed to a couple of doors to the left of the hall "This is where the members and guests can access the pools and beach area. Come along everyone, your training buddies are waiting for you down in the staff room." We followed her through door that read **Staff Only**, down a flight of stairs to a room with lockers, tables and chairs. At the far side of the room sat 5 people in uniforms, all chatting. As they caught sight of Mrs. Snorff, the chatter stopped and they stood up. Mrs. Snorff cleared her throat, more likely to get everyone's attention, than for the sake of needing to clear her windpipe. "When I call your name you will go and join your training buddy. Please pay attention I don't want to have to do this twice".

I looked at all the trainers; they couldn't be much older than most of us. One male trainer was craning his neck to get a good look at all the new meat; another one just leaned against the lockers as if he was totally bored with the whole process. One of the female trainers had a very pleasant, kind looking face. I hoped I would have her; with one of my sisters, that would be perfect. Mrs. Snorff began, "The first group of two will be training with Ian Smith in the guest lounge upstairs". As soon as she mentioned his name, the boy that was leaning against the lockers stepped forward to assess the group of us a little more carefully. Mrs. Snorff continued, "Carly Anderson and Fina Terra, please go and stand with Ian now". My heart skipped a beat as I could sense that all the colour that may have been left in my face was now gone. I felt a smack of panic deep within my chest. I needed to be with one of my sisters; how could I make this known if Aella and I were separated too? Could I find the words to speak up or maybe Aella would do it for me. My mind was racing. I took a deep breathe to slowly calm my breathing, but it didn't do as much good as I had hoped. "Kailey Angel will be taking the next group of two to work in our housekeeping department," Mrs. Snorff said. "Naida Terra and Aella Terra, please join Kailey". As I looked over at the girl named Kailey, I was pleasantly relieved to find it was the kind looking girl that I had hoped for. I let out a sign of relief and followed my sister to our spot beside Kailey. "Hey, welcome!...We are going to have so much fun," Kailey giggled.

The rest of the group was divided up accordingly, but to be perfectly honest, I didn't really pay much attention. I was just so relieved to be with my sister, that I didn't care too much about the rest. When Mrs. Snorff finished dividing everyone up, she addressed the groups. "Please pay close attention to your trainers, you only get a couple of days of hands-on training. After which you will be put on the schedule with your own shifts. Our trainers will show you the rest of the facilities that we didn't see on our tour. Please stay to the staff areas as much as possible, unless your position dictates otherwise. When in the presence of the guests, always be polite and helpful. Good Luck everyone, and don't forget to smile." With that she hurried off through the doorway of the staffroom. We broke up into our smaller groups. I saw Fina talking with the others in her group she glanced over and smiled. I knew she would be fine on her own. She mouthed something that looked like *"See you at the end of the day"*. She turned and followed Carly and Ian out of the doorway. We turned back to look at Kailey; she stood with a bright smile on face "Okay you two let's get started. I think we should go and get your uniforms down the hall from laundry before we begin with our first room." Oddly enough I felt pretty comfortable around Kailey; she seemed carefree and eager. Aella asked, "Have you worked here long?"

"For the last 3 summers. It's a great job and the social life isn't half bad either," Kailey answered letting a grin part her lips. "Just wait 'til Ian, oh you know the guy that was just here a few minutes ago. Wait until he organizes the first staff bonfire of the summer…You'll love it."

"The staff gets pretty…*close* here." I detected a double meaning in her answer, but I didn't really understand it.

After we picked up our uniforms Kailey gave Aella and I moment to get into our dresses in the staff washroom. As I came out of my stall where I had been changing, Aella looked at me and smiled, "Nice outfit; I hope Fina's is as beautiful. I would hate for her to miss out on this." I glanced into the mirror on the wall. The plain blue polyester blend pants, with elastic waistband, seemed to hang off my hips, but the smock-like shirt at least hung low enough that it hid the waistband of the pants. Somehow the outfit looked better on Kailey then it did on either of us. Aella and I threw our clothes in a locker and met Kailey just outside the staffroom. We followed Kailey back down the hall where she introduced us to our supervisor, Mrs. Blackwell.

Mrs. Blackwell welcomed us to her department. She handed us nametags and gave Kailey a list of rooms to get to work on. "These rooms had early check outs, so you can get started on them. Kailey, make sure you show the girls where to get the trolley, dear." Mrs. Blackwell flashed a smile at the three of us and wished us well as we hurried off. The three of us walked down to another room to pick up a cleaning trolley. Kailey showed us how to stock the things we needed, and in no time we were on our way.

Kailey lead us to a elevator marked SERVICE and pressed the button. The doors opened immediately, and we loaded the elevator with the three of us and the trolley. We only went two floors up; it appeared that's all there was. The doors from the elevator opened up to another service hallway. "Come on this way," Kailey said as she pushed through another door. Aella pushed the trolley as we entered the guest area. It was beautiful. The carpet was red with black and gold detail, while the walls seem to warm the visitors with an inviting shade of beige.

There was a sharp tug on my arm as I realized I had been standing staring again. Aella pulled me along in step so I could keep from tripping while I looked around until finally she found it too difficult to push the trolley and pull me, while keeping pace with Kailey. "Naida, please....!!!" she stressed. Just then Kailey found the first room and we went to work on it. I was lucky. It wasn't facing the ocean so I managed to stay focused on what Kailey had to teach us. Kailey was good; she worked quickly, but was meticulous about the room. She said we had to be thorough. Though Mrs. Blackwell was very nice, she also had high expectations of how the rooms should look when we were finished.

The day seemed to move faster. I almost forgot about being nervous. By the time we finished our last room, I was tired. Kailey looked at her watch and said, "Hey, thanks for being such fast learners. Let's get the trolley back downstairs and we can punch out for the day."

Once we were back in the staffroom Kailey said, "I'll meet you here tomorrow at 9:00 am, Okay?"

"Sounds great, thank you Kailey", Aella said and we both smiled at Kailey's eager face.

"Bye for now" Kailey turned and joined a couple of other girls chatting at one of the tables. "Bye" I said, now getting a little eager myself to get home. She turned back and tossed a smile at the two of us.

We met Fina in front of the Beach Club and started walking home. Fina filled us in on the details of her day in the lounge, telling us about the people she was working with, and some of the guests in the lounge she had served. This was a prefect job for her. She had so much confidence. I knew she would do well, and it sounded fantastic. I was so lost in her stories that I hadn't realized how close we were to home. As we crested the hill, I saw the ocean with the little cottage near it. Mother was waiting outside. The ocean was moving in a way that anyone looking at it would have thought it was just welcoming, but I knew it had missed me the way I had missed it all day. I broke into a light jog, but clearly that wasn't enough; faster and faster I ran. My eyes fixed on one thing, the only thing I truly needed. I kicked off my shoes, almost dumping myself into the sand. Seconds later I dove. As my flesh became one with the salt water, I felt my physical body dissolving. Like a clump of salt into water I was nothing more than a thought. Moving through the waves and with the waves, as I had done for so many centuries before. I was *home*.

CHAPTER 3

Secrets Revealed

I soared through my ocean for hours gaining energy as I went. I knew the longer I stayed, the less I would want to go back to the cottage with my make-believe family. But we needed each other and our goal was clear. I just wished that I didn't have to leave the ocean to do it. As I sailed along dipping and diving amongst the very active sea life, I knew they felt a sense of relief at having me back in their waters as well.

I was aware of a gentle breeze up on the surface of the water as I allowed my thoughts to surface above the water. The breeze spoke to me. "Having fun?" I knew this voice, for it had been with me for as long as I have been with the water.

"Hello, Aella. I should ask you the same question. Is Mother upset with me? I didn't give Mother the opportunity to stop me on the beach earlier," I said.

"Don't kid yourself Naida. If Mother wanted to stop you, your physical little human butt would have been still on the sand. No, she expected this, and knew you would need time to recharge your energy. However, day will break soon on our beach and you need to be back before that happens." Aella finished in a much more serious tone than she had started with.

"I understand but aren't the waters of Bermuda beautiful at this time of night?" I was just testing to see how soon she was meaning. I had no idea how long I had been gone for. Time was one thing I never worried about, at least until just recently.

"Now Naida!" Aella replied yet a little stronger than before. "The waters of Bermuda are beautiful, but you need to be in a Cottage on a beach in Nova Scotia right now," she finished.

"Alright then but will you glide with me" I knew she was enjoying the energy in which she got from the wind, as much as I was enjoying mine from the water. We sailed back to our beach in silence, both of us just enjoying our existence. I could only guess how long it took us to return, but we made it back before the sun crested the horizon.

Mother had left clothes for us on the rocks by the trees. There was a spot just down from the cottage, past the gentle sands of the beach where a cluster of trees grew close to the water's edge. Several large rocks had accumulated there, and it made for a somewhat private spot to form my human body and dress it. As I washed up onto the rocks, parting from my source, I felt my body forming. Within seconds my being was covered with flesh. Watching the last couple of fingers grow into their physical state, I felt a slight chill of the cool morning air brush my skin. Then I could feel that I was fully formed. But before I could pull on all of my clothes. I was covered in goose bumps. "Aella, next time we leave our sources, could you warm yours up a bit." I winked at Aella and she just laughed.

Once Aella and I were dressed, we sat for a moment on the sand in front of our cottage enjoying our recent surge of energy. None of us needed food; the physical human form of energy. Only our sources could provide the energy we needed. We ate food in order to appear normal, as normal as we could hope to look in our physical bodies, anyway.

I lay back quietly relaxed now. "Ah, I feel so good."

"I bet our new jobs at the Beach Club will be easier for you to handle today, too," Aella said. I had forgotten about that; we had to go again today. A slight shudder ran down my spine, but then the thought of my night in the water seemed to invigorate me again. "I think you're right," I replied softly.

After a couple of minutes Aella and I thought we should return to the cottage before Mother had to come looking for us. We entered the cottage to find Mother standing by the fireplace looking as if she were in the middle of an argument. I glanced around the cottage but couldn't find Fina anywhere. Mother said, still not acknowledging that Aella and I had entered the room, "We will talk about this later". I opened my mouth to speak when I realize Mother still wasn't addressing us. Two seconds later, Fina sat on the floor, naked beside the fireplace, and I realized Fina had been with her energy source also. Their argument was likely similar to the one I thought about having with Aella in the waters of Bermuda earlier. None of us liked to ever leave our sources for too long. With a huff, Fina pulled on her work uniform that was neatly folded beside the fireplace.

"Welcome back girls, do you feel better?" Mother's voice was softer than before. I ran over and threw my arms around her.

"Oh Mother, Thank you for not objecting with last night. I feel wonderful".

Mother's face was soft and warm now all tones of upset were gone. "Well, the people of Nova Scotia can relax today as I am sure the oceans will calm and the winds gentle. We'll just have to hope there aren't any brush fires on your way to work" Mother smiled and threw a glance at Fina, now doing her hair in the mirror.

"Don't tempt me Mother Terra" Fina said with a devious smile.

Within a few minutes the three of us were on the beach walking up the hill to go to work, away from our little cottage and my adored ocean.

The week seemed to whiz by. Each day I became more and more comfortable in my new surroundings. Kailey and I were a housekeeping team now, and Aella was paired up with a lady that was probably 20 years our physical senior. But Aella could relate to anyone, and within the first day together, Aella and Mary were working as though they had always been a team. It had actually been Aella's choice, when Mrs. Blackwell had said that they needed to break us up into twos. I thought Aella had exploded, she volunteered so fast. It wasn't that Aella didn't like Kailey; it was just that she knew I was just getting comfortable with Kailey, and Aella didn't want to see me having to switch.

Fina was enjoying her job in the lounge, with one exception. Fina found it very difficult to focus on the beach club's guests when, each day around 11 o'clock the bartenders lit the fire in the lounge fireplace. We all loved our individual sources and could somewhat control how we addressed them during the day. Nevertheless, the pull Fina felt when close to the *birth of a new fire* was an immense strain on her. Because of this, she had dropped a tray of cocktail glasses and broken 3 plates that were full of food. Fina determined by the end of the week, it was just safer and easier for her to excuse her self to the ladies room when she saw the bartender head over with the matches.

Fina said that there were two bartenders that worked in the lounge. Ian worked the day shift, and Cody worked the evening shift. I had never seen Cody, but by the way the girls in the staffroom talked about him, he was apparently quite good looking. Kailey just laughed at the other girls, and said stuff like, "You may think he's hot, but try living with him everyday," or "Hot and smelly". Kailey loved her brother, but like any little sister she had to have her comments too. They were actually a lot closer than she let on. You could tell by the tone in her voice, she always had her comments light and joking and loving. Kailey told me that she had just turned 18, and Cody was 20. He was a University student, but that was all I knew about him. Kailey was very excited to be starting University in the fall. I found her life to be so fascinating. I just let her talk as much as she wanted. I don't know if she thought it was odd or not, but every time she would try to change the subject to me, I would shift it back to her.

Early Friday morning Kailey and I were asked to clean the Beach Club entrance in the front lobby. So we grabbed our cleaning trolley and headed to the front. While Kailey set to work on the reception desk, I started cleaning the glass shelves over by the lobby's entrance. The shelves had been pushed up against a window to the right of the doorway. Spraying, wiping, cleaning each of the 10 shelves, I had gotten pretty focused on getting it clean, when I became aware of a set of eyes on the other side of the window outside. I lifted my gaze to meet the one staring at me. The eyes that I met with made me gasp. They were of the deepest brown, with the warmth of 12 wool blankets, the honesty of a newborn child, and the depth and passion of a thousand untold nights. My eyes seemed locked, as if it were a place they had longed to be. A familiar warmth traveled through my body, causing my head to take flight. I struggled to break my gaze from these eyes. Then appeared a beautiful mouth that seemed to hold my eyes, not quite as strongly as the eyes had, but it too, made it hard to look away. As I focused on this mouth, it broke open into the most heavenly smile. My knees were weak and my head was still spinning. What was this? What was happening to me? My heart raced and my cheeks filled with blood. As my breath became shallow, I became aware, only for a moment, of yells and screams coming from the direction of the lounge area. No matter how hard I tried, I couldn't break my gaze that was now back upon the eyes. Suddenly, the room started to spin and within a couple of heartbeats I was on the floor. Though everything was black, I could still see the eyes as if they had been burned into my retinas. Lost in what seemed to be a dream state, I felt warm, safe and comfortable, as if at home in my ocean. I felt as though everything was suspended ~ time, life, the entire world and all the concerns that went with it. As if my aquatic world was happy, and all had been put right again. The eyes comforted me in my darkness as they seemed to lessen my burden of what brought me to these shores in the first place. So warm, so happy, so…safe! I drifted, enjoying all of these things in what could have been a dream, but felt more like a memory. Moments later, though I can't be sure how long exactly, I heard Kailey from somewhere beside me. "Naida! Naida! Can you hear me?" her voice seemed distance for a moment until I heard another voice.

"Naida? Is that you? What's happened are you alright?" I tried to open my eyes, though a part of me just wanted to stay with those eyes there in the darkness…just the two of us. While the other side of me continued to force my eyes open, they finally flickered into focus. I became aware of Kailey sitting beside me on the floor, while Fina stood over me with a serious look in her eyes. I was pretty sure I hadn't been on the floor that long, but how was it that Fina knew to look for me? My head stopped spinning and Kailey realized my sister looked as though she should be the one by my side. Kailey excused her self and allowed my sister to take her place. "Fina, can I get her anything?" Kailey said with such concern in her voice.

"No but perhaps you can help me get her to her feet." Fina said softly to Kailey.

Fina and Kailey helped me to my feet, "I've got it from here, thank you, Kailey." Fina had very politely dismissed Kailey so that we would be able to speak freely. Fina took me over to the Ladies washroom which was just through the lounge. It wasn't until we got to the lounge that I realized how Fina had known that something had happened to me. One look at the ocean and I understood the reason for the screams that I had heard earlier. Waves were almost 30 feet tall, slamming down onto the shoreline. Thank goodness it was too early in the day for the beach to be crowded. I would imagine that anyone who had been out there had run into the beach club for safe measure. Safely inside the Ladies room, Fina put a cool hand towel on my forehead. I looked into her eyes and asked, "What was that? One minute I was looking into some ones eyes and the next minute I was flat on my butt." Fina's look hardened slightly, "Someone's eyes…" she repeated. "It was a boy, a BOY…you let a boy cause a natural disaster Naida!?" Fina was always a little dramatic.

I still wasn't on the same page as her, but I had a feeling she was about to enlighten me. Just then a young woman came running into the washroom. "Wow, did you see that? One minute I'm picking up beautiful shells from the shoreline, the next minute waves are crashing everywhere around me. I don't even know how I got back to the Club with getting swept away." She glanced into the mirror, then disappeared into a bathroom stall. Obviously, her adrenaline hadn't worn off yet.

Fina shot me another look much more steely than the last. "Are you okay to return to work now Naida?" Fina asked, a little intolerantly. I nodded my head yes, and pushed open the bathroom door. As Fina and I walked through the lounge to the stairs back to the lobby, I stole another glance at my ocean. Just as I was now calming down, so was it. However, all the people in the lounge were talking about it. They were standing by the windows staring out to see if it would start up again.

Kailey was waiting for me in the lobby as I walked down the stairs. Fina called from the lounge, "I'll see you after work," assuring me that our conversation from the washroom wasn't yet over.

"Naida!" Kailey came running over, "Are you alright? Do you need some water or anything?" Kailey had such a look of concern on her face. She had no idea how much I needed *some water*, but not the water to which she was referring. I needed my salt water. I didn't really answer her; so she didn't say much more about it.

The rest of the day crept along painfully and slowly, partially because I was concerned about the conversation that would be held in the small cottage on the beach tonight. In addition, my thoughts kept drifting back to what Fina had said, *"A BOY"*. Is that what I was gazing at in the window before everything went weird? Those eyes belonged to a boy.

After lunch I suppose Kailey thought enough time had passed regarding the morning events, so she quietly said, "Hey Naida, did you meet my brother this morning? He came in right after you…oh I guess not, sorry. He brought me my lunch that I had forgotten at home this morning. I need to introduce you to him, soon." Could *the boy* be the same person as this Cody, Kailey's older brother? Oh boy!

I threw a half smile her way and directed the conversation to something a little lighter. "So, I heard some of the girls in the lunchroom talking about Ian's staff bonfire. What is that all about?"

Kailey's face became excited "Oh ya, it's next Friday night…a week tonight. Are you and your sisters coming? Hey, I've got a great idea, how about I pick you up? My parents are letting me have the car Friday night 'cause they know the party will go pretty late. They said I can drive Cody home after his shift, too."

I hesitated for a moment "Well, I would need to check with my Moth…I mean my Mom. Can I get back to you?" If *the boy* was in fact Kailey's brother, then he no doubt was planning on bringing his eyes to work with him, and at some point I would have to look at them again. In which case, was I about to drown the entire staff at the party?

CHAPTER 4

The Talk

Fina and Aella were waiting for me at the front of the beach club at the end of the day. Judging by the look on Aella's face, Fina had wasted no time in filling Aella in on the details of this morning. Aella watched me walk through the door and over to them. "Hey, how was your day?" As if she didn't already know.

"Do you think Mother knows yet?" I said. And both of my sisters nodded their headed *yes*. I already knew the answer, I had just been hopeful. Mother would have sensed the waves, if she hadn't seen them for herself. The walk home was quiet and slow. They knew I was nervous and like any good supportive sisters would do, they dragged their heels, too.

As we crested the hill I prepared myself for what I was sure would come. My eyes met the upset ocean water at once as it churned and peaked; it was anxious. As soon as my shoes came in contact with the sand, it was if the sand had a mind of its own. It rolled in such a way that it carried me to the door of the cottage much faster than I would have walked to it. "Get in here Naida", I heard from behind the door. My sisters were still running to catch up to me. I pushed the door open to meet a hard icy stare from Mother.

An hour went by. She was just as enraged as the moment I walked in. "What did you think you were doing today? What if someone had gotten hurt, like that girl on the beach? As it was I had to shield her from the waves until the poor thing caught on that she would drown if she didn't move inside." *That's* how I hadn't harmed her; Mother had been able to protect her.

Finally, after another hour, Mother started to lose her wind enough so that we could discuss how to prevent this from happening again. "A boy" Mother repeated over and over "Fina, did you see which boy it was?"

"Yes Mother" Fina hesitated for a moment "His name is Cody Angel, he is the brother of the young lady that Naida works with". My heart sank; how was I to continue on with our plan if I couldn't look certain people in the face. Was it just Cody, or would there be others?

"I need some time to think about this girls and to consult with the Connected Ones. I will be back in a while," Mother said slowly, as if deep in thought. Her eyes appeared glazed and unfocused now. No longer looking at us anymore, we knew she was already looking for answers. We knew that all humans were connected, but the humans that Mother sought could hear us better than the others, and had been able to communicate with Mother for centuries. Aella, Fina and I all froze for a minute wondering if this was a cruel joke, and Mother was going to start yelling again. But she didn't, and we didn't give her a second minute to change her mind. I was the first one out the door with Aella and Fina hot on my heels.

This time I was careful to strip off by the trees, neatly folding my clothes on the rock before I dove into the water. Dissolving into the water as I had done every night this week, I could feel my energy being fed now. I heard the whisper from the breeze above, "We shouldn't go too far tonight, I told Fina the same thing. When Mother is ready she will need us back right away. Fina is lighting a fire on the shore now, she will feel better soon, too. Enjoy!!" and with that said, Aella was gone to enjoy her time with her source.

It wasn't too long before I heard Mother, as though she were a thought inside my head. "Come back now, girls". Within moments we were all on the beach together. We sat down around the fire Fina had just come out of. Mother began with a great sigh. "Naida, this boy is very important to us. You must control what is most natural to you. Can you try?"

I looked around the circle "I will" I reply reluctantly.

"It's not going to be easy Naida. Don't think I don't understand that. When you accepted this task, you knew of some of the challenges. It would seem you are faced with some of them now. You must stay focused on the success of your task, and find a way to control the way he makes you feel. You must learn from this experience so the outcome is not so devastating, and learn it quickly for the sake of all the life on this coast." Mother stood back letting her words sink in, and then she seemed to remember something. "Now, Fina mentioned a party of sorts next Friday. Will this boy be there?"

I cleared my throat "According to Kailey his sister, he's working until 2:00 am, but he will join the party likely for a bit after his shift."

"Perfect," Mother said. "By then the numbers of people should be less, and it will give Naida a chance to *control herself*. I will be near should something go…*wrong*." Mother finished.

"Mother I don't understand. Why would we continue when there is so much to lose?" I said slowly.

"My dear Naida …there is so much more to lose if we don't continue." Mother said firmly. "The connected ones said this is important so you need to focus and find a way to deal with this quickly."

"But Mother ..." I started but Mother spoke over my voice.

"No more Naida your path has been chosen, so find a way to walk it." Mother stood up and walked back to the cottage, making it very clear that this conversation was over. A moment after I heard the cottage door shut, Fina jumped to her feet and started pulling her cloths off again.

Before she could get too far, Aella grabbed her arm, "Fina we have to be back at work soon, there's no time."

But Fina knew differently, pulling her arm from Aella's grip. "Yes there is, we get days off you know, and today is one of them." Fina wasn't wasting anymore time chatting; she smiled and disappeared into the fire.

Great! So now I had a week to worry whether I would end up killing all the staff at the Beach Club. I couldn't help but wonder what I had seen in Cody's eyes that made me react so severely. Aella could see I was paining over Mother's decision, so she tried to take my mind off of it. "Come on, Fina's got a point, let's be ourselves for while." I knew exactly what she meant, and it sounded good to me. "Naida, take some time and enjoy being home with your ocean family. Find the strength within them to help feed your strength to walk your path as a human. I'll meet you back here tomorrow night. Be safe; I think I'll feed Fina's fire with a couple more logs before I go.'
"Okay Aella, thank you." With a heavy heart and much on my mind, I got to my feet and undressed by the trees again. Without even a splash I was home again.

CHAPTER 5

Introduction

My sisters and I arrived at work a little earlier than usual on Monday. We went down to the staff room together to put our things away in the lockers. Fina decided to head upstairs to clean the bar area before Ian got in. She waved a warm good bye and threw us a smile as she ducked out the door.

Aella and I sat quietly for a moment. Then Aella said as she picked up my hand from the table, "You keep worrying like that and you will have aged yourself so much, you'll be able to retire at the end of this summer." It didn't help but I laughed anyway. As Mary entered the staffroom Aella let my hand go. If Mary hadn't known we were sisters, she might have thought she was interrupting a *private moment*. I smiled and laughed to myself; people were so funny about love. Aella smiled and shot me a wink; I think she was thinking the same thing.

"Hi Mary, did you have a nice evening Saturday night?" Aella said cheerfully as she skipped over to Mary's side. "Oh yes, thank you for asking, our 15th wedding anniversary was wonderful. Wait until you see the string of pearls Carlton got for me. Beautiful, Beautiful!" she repeated in an excited manner. Aella shot me a look to keep my mouth shut; she must have known what was running through my head. *Beautiful, I bet, but*

TIDES

not his to give; they belonged to my friends in the ocean, even if he had paid some guy for them. When Mary had finished putting her things away, they to left the room to start their rounds. "Bye, Naida" they waved as they left together.

"See you later", I called after them.

Several people were now quickly in and out of their lockers. I glanced at the clock on the wall, starting to wonder were Kailey had gotten to. Just as I was about to go and grab the trolley, and start on my own, in ran Kailey. With red cheeks and out of breath, it looked as though she had just run some sort of race. "Kailey!" I called out, relief in my voice.

The instant she laid eyes on me the biggest smile lit up her face. "Hi!! Oh-my-gosh I have *so* much to tell you! Help me get ready so I can get to it", Kailey breathed anxiously. I jumped from my seat and helped her stow her things in her locker. "Hurry, or we will be late getting our trolley". We bolted down the hall to check in with Mrs. Blackwell.

She was already standing there with our trolley and rooms list, "Hurry up girls, get started please" she said curtly. I took the list and Kailey took the trolley.

When we were safely out of ear shot through the back halls and elevator Kailey said, "The first room is just up here, let's get there first."

I opened the door to the room and Kailey parked the trolley in front. We walked in with some cleaning supplies from the trolley. Once inside the door Kailey's face lit up again as if she were a fire that someone had just thrown some gasoline on. "I had an hour and a half inquisition period with my brother last night about you!" as if it were a grand finale.

My mouth dropped open "Pardon?"

"Okay" Kailey began a little slower this time "Do you remember Friday when you were…eye locked with my brother in the front window?"

Wasn't anyone going to let me forget that, I sighed "Yes".

"Well, apparently at first he thought you were me, seeing that we have the same uniforms, I guess. He was going to scare me through the window by putting his face really close to it, and when I went to see what was staring at me he was just going to make a face or something *really mature*" her sarcasm oozed. She continued "Except you got him; I mean, he looked into your eyes and ..." she trailed off. "Well, the next minute you were on the floor, people were screaming in the lounge. I didn't know what was going on, but once your sister came over I thought I should back off and leave you to her. I went over to talk to my brother. I told you that he had come to bring me my lunch that I had forgotten at home. Well, by the time I got home Sunday night from my friend Leslie's house, Cody had a billion questions about you and ..." she trailed off again. However, this time her cheeks were flushed and clearly she was embarrassed.

I smiled, and with a little giggle I said, "What is it?"

She took a deep breath. "I realized, I don't know a lot about *you*. I think I have told you everything about me. I feel like I've been so rude but I don't know much about you! I'm so sorry, I hope you haven't been thinking I'm the rudest person on the planet."

I started laughing out loud, poor Kailey had know idea I had been making her talk about herself on purpose. "Oh Kailey," still laughing a little, "Of course I don't think that; I love hearing all about you. You are so much fun to be with. Please don't think that ever again." I finished with a smile.

"It's just, the last time I saw Cody this jacked up about a girl ..." she paused for a moment. "No, let me rephrase that. The last time I saw Cody this jacked up," a huge smile consumed her face, "was about a fish."

I dropped my cleaning rag and my face turned red. In a small voice I said "A fish?"

This time Kailey was the one laughing out loud. "Well, it wasn't actually one fish, it was many fish." She laughed still enjoying the joke that I didn't understand. "It was the night that he received the letter accepting him into the Marine Biology course at Dalhousie University.

Suddenly, I could feel the pulse of my heartbeat in my cheeks and my head start to spin, I knew all too well what the ocean would be doing in a moment if I didn't try to control this feeling. I thought to myself, *slow down, breathe in and out, think about…hmm my favorite whale family that I love swimming with. Oh yes that's it, as I let out a sigh, much better.* I think I controlled that pretty well, I thought approvingly to myself. At least I didn't have to fear Mother, tonight.

The next couple of days went by pretty uneventfully, which I was not complaining about. Kailey talked on and on about her brother, filling me in on his life. I gave her some sketchy details about my life just enough to keep him asking Kailey for more, until we could hopefully meet on Friday night.

…

It was Wednesday now, and Kailey and I were just about finished for the day. I grabbed the garbage that we had collected over the course of the day from the rooms and said, "Kailey, I'll meet you in the staffroom. I'm just going to run the garbage out to the garbage room."

"Okay. See you there. I'll return the trolley," she answered back.

I set off down the hall to the staff only corridor. However, I only got 10 feet in when I was halted by a skid on wheels filled with cases of beer which blocked the entire width of the corridor. I couldn't see a way around it, or over it, but someone was taking the cases off the skid and putting them into the walk-in fridge next to it. So I waited until I could see someone. Finally, a case at eye level was taken off the top and the person removing the cases froze as I did.

Those eyes again, but this time the lips beneath them spoke to me. "Hi, Naida." Oh boy; he just spoke to me and my mouth and brain just shut down. My pulse quickened and my face flushed—must think of the whales, yes the whales, whales, whales, whales I repeated in my head. "Hi, Cody." My voice cracked, I'm such a geek I thought to myself.

"Can I help you?" he said smiling.

"Yes...Whales agh I mean garbage, I have garbage I need to put in the garbage room." His beautiful smile turned into a light chuckle as he reached his arm through the break in the case.

"Here, hand it to me and I will put it in the garbage room." I smiled yet still focusing on the whales in my head as I passed the garbage through to him. "Thanks" I said softy.

As I turned to go he called, "Hey, I'll see you Friday night at the bonfire. I hear Kailey's offered to drive you home, too." He flashed a smile and my heart skipped.

"See you then," I answered, still focusing on Whales.

When I got back to the staffroom Kailey and Aella were waiting for me. "What took you so long?" Kailey blurted out.

"Some guys were unloading a skid of beer and I couldn't get by until one of them offered to help me". I said as causally as possible.

Kailey's face lit up again as she put two and two together, and came up with the answer of Cody to her equation. "You met then, did you?" she smiled.

Aella looked a little confused "Who did you meet?"

I hesitated for a moment but Kailey jumped right in, "Cody, my brother".

Aella's head whipped around, "You meet Cody today? Now?!"

I smiled and threw her a wink "Yup," and while Kailey's head was turned to her locker I said quietly, "and I did pretty well, I think." Though I hadn't spoken to Fina yet, who would have had a clear view of the tides during my encounter, I'm sure I would hear soon enough how well I actually had managed. The three of us walked out of the staff room talking about my resent encounter with Cody. Kailey was so happy I had finally met him that it was hard for her to sound casual about the meeting.

Finally we reached the front of the Beach Club were Fina met us. Fina's face had a very interesting look upon. The three of us said good-bye to Kailey and we set off towards home. Fina waited until Kailey was out of earshot. "So Naida…anything to tell me about today?" she gazed into my eyes as I skipped along beside her, feeling unusually light and happy.

"Why do you ask?" I replied.

"Oh Naida…just fill her in. For goodness sake—she met Cody today!" Aella couldn't wait for me to open my mouth so I shot her a look, but honestly I didn't care.

"Well, I kind of knew already." Fina began when I cut in, "No-o-o-o, did I hurt anyone?" I had been feeling so proud of myself for controlling my emotions that I was sure that Fina wouldn't have noticed anything with the tides. I guess I didn't do as well as I had thought.

"Actually …" the edges of Fina's lips curled up into a half smile "it was Cody that gave it away. He and Ian were talking by the bar as I was cleaning up. You definitely have his attention." She winked at me and threw her head back with a loud roar of laughter. "Sounds like he's pretty hooked. He was telling Ian to keep an eye on you at the bonfire before he gets off work. Cody doesn't want any other guy moving in on you before he has a chance to get there. So Naida, you better behave yourself or this could turn ugly."

"That's enough Fina, now you're starting to embarrassed me," I said softly. The rest of the way home I thought about how well I had controlled myself. How *maybe,* I wouldn't end up drowning the entire party on Friday night.

As soon as we crested the hill near the cottage, my feet hit the sand running. I needed to be with my ocean for a while.

CHAPTER 6

Friday Night

"Fina, you look amazing! How did you do that with your hair?" Aella said with a tone of admiration.

"Thank you…but you don't really want to know," Fina said with a very sly smile as she returned to the mirror. "Hurry up you guys, Kailey will be here soon and we don't want to keep her waiting". I was wearing a pair of lose-fitting jeans, my favorite t-shirt, and a University sweatshirt that Mother thought would make me look a little more in tune with the group.

There was a knock on the door and my heart skipped a beat. I knew it would be Kailey at the door, but she was just the start to the evening, the same evening I knew I had to keep so under control. "Come on in" Mother said as she pushed the door open for Kailey.

"Good Evening Mrs. Terra, How are you this evening?" Kailey smiled shyly.

"Very well, Kailey but please call me Anna. The girls have spoken so highly of you since they started working at the club. I feel like you are one of the family already," Mother said warmly.

Kailey looked around, in her cheery sparkling voice and said, "I love your place. It is so…inviting."

"Thanks Kailey …" Aella snickered as she threw an arm around Mother and winked at me, "Let's get going." Everyone laughed. We could all feel Kailey's excitement building to get going to the party.

"Don't wait up. We will likely be very late." Fina said as she reached for the door.

"Drive carefully," I knew Mother only threw that in 'cause it sounded like something a Mother would say to her children as they left for an evening of fun. I laughed under my breath.

As we all piled into Kailey's parent's Prius, Kailey grabbed my arm just before I followed my sisters in. "Hey Naida, just a sec," she said reluctantly. I frowned a little, sensing that something was bothering her.

"Of course Kailey, what's up?"

She sighed a little as she began slowly, "Cody is a really sweet guy, but two years ago, just before he started University, he sort of…broke up with his girlfriend. I haven't seen him this excited to see some one in awhile so …" she trailed off for only moment. "Well, if you're not interested in him, could you—I don't know, just be nice but honest."

My eyes didn't leave hers and I couldn't believe my ears. She had no idea how he made me feel. "Kailey" I began in a very soft, small voice, "I will be nice 'cause I'd really want to get to know your brother better." Now with broad smiles across both our faces I tossed an arm around her and said, "Getting a little protective aren't we?" We both laughed as we hopped into the car. But I got her point, and she knew it.

By the time the four of us rounded the boathouse, we could see the huge flames from the bonfire as if they were lashing at the wind. I looked at Fina and could see her eyes yearn for her source, and then suddenly they became quite steely. I grabbed her hand for a moment and gave it a squeeze. We both had something to control tonight. Let's hope no one would catch on to our personal crusades, for if they did, it would mean we failed in one way or another.

As the party got into full swing, my two sisters mingled. With Kailey by my side, I actually got a chance to meet a lot of people I had only see in the staffroom, but had never actually spoken to. I was starting to have fun as the night went on. Apparently, Ian was hitting on Fina. It kind of looked funny from where we were standing, because he had thrown an arm around Fina as if it was a causal, friendly thing to do while talking to a group of co-workers. The only face I recognized in that group was Carly, the girl that Fina had trained with. Fina's face was somewhat relaxed, but she was not really paying much attention to Ian. No, you could see she wasn't going to drop her guard being so close to the fire now. I knew she wanted to be near it, as she would be able to feel the fire's energy warming her, which she would enjoy. However, if she were to falter and allow the pull to win, there would be no amount of explaining that could get us out of that one. She had controlled the initial pull, when she first saw the flames, and it wasn't like this was her first time resisting the natural urge. Fina was pretty good at controlling her desire. She had taught me so much in the past several weeks.

Kailey and I stood talking to a couple of other housekeepers who were our age when I felt an arm slip onto my shoulder. As my heart skipped and I could smell different cologne in the air; I knew it wasn't Aella coming over to say *hi*. "Hello, Ladies. Is everyone enjoying their evening?" I still hadn't turned to look at the face that belonged to that warm voice. However, judging by the looks on the girl's faces across from Kailey and I, they looked as if they would take my place in a heartbeat. My heart began to race and my breath was shallow, the warmth from his hand on my shoulder was so…comfortable.

Kailey spoke in her cheery voice, "Hey Cody, you've met my friend and co-worker," she giggled at the formality of her words, "Naida. And this is Arlene and Janie. They work with us in housekeeping." She seemed to finish the latter of the introduction quickly, so as not to take to much attention away from our introduction.

"Hello." I could see out of the corner of my eye that he was nodding at the girls however; he gave my shoulder a gentle squeeze and left his arm comfortably around me.

Okay, I was doing pretty well. The ocean in front of us was only churning slightly more than before. I would have to meet his eyes soon, but maybe I could put it off for a little while longer.

"Hi" I glanced up focusing on his lips rather than his eyes. They split into a heavenly smile before I could drop my gaze. I breathed deeply, *Whales* now running through my head. I'm good, really good.

"Come sit with me over by the fire," he was only referring to Kailey and I as he finished with "It was really nice to meet you ladies. Have a wonderful night." As he nodded again to Arlene and Janie, they smiled, not seeming to mind the way he just dismissed them from our conversation.

"That was rude Cody", Kailey piped up once we were out of the girl's earshot.

"They didn't seem to mind but if you would like to go back and continue your conversation with them Kailey, I won't stand in your way." He paused for a short moment, "However I may stand in Naida's way." He now had a very confident tone in his voice and I thought it's now or never. I lifted my eyes to meet his, and somehow the light from the bonfire made it difficult to see the depth of those beautiful brown eyes. It was there, but not as striking as it had been in the daylight a week ago.

The ocean was still churning, but it was manageable. I might not drown everyone tonight.

The three of us joined the group of kids Ian and Fina were with. We talked as a group for an hour or so before couples started trailing off down the beach. I looked around for Aella for a moment before I found her talking with Mary and her husband. They seemed to be engaged in quite the conversation so I turned back to our group. It was now rather small; the only ones left were Fina, Ian, Carly, Cody, Kailey and myself. I was getting a little anxious now. It was getting really late and Cody and I hadn't had any time to talk, just the two of us, like I had hoped. Actually, I had been dreading it, but now I was feeling pretty confident, which came as a surprise to me.

Cody cleared his throat "Ian, you need any help cleaning up?"
"No thanks, Fina has offered to help. I'm going to drive her home after." His mouth turned up into a sly little smile. "Okay well, I'm going to get the rest of the girls home, I think." Said Cody. Kailey was half asleep in the chair next to me when she said with a sigh, "Can you drive though; I'm to tired?"

"I think I would feel more comfortable with that right now" as he took the keys from her out stretch hand.

After we got Aella, we all walked to the car together. Just before we reached the car, Cody threw his arm around me again. My heart skipped as he gently pulled my head close to his face. I could feel his warm breath in my ear, sending shivers down my neck. "Would it be alright with you if I dropped my sister at home first, before I drive you and Aella home? It will just take a moment more."

I felt like I was a puddle of water on the ground; my knees were gone and my head spun for a moment—Whales, Whales, Whales I repeated in my head. "Sure," I managed to say in a low, quiet voice.

About 10 minutes later, Aella, Cody and I walked towards the small cottage on the beach. Cody reached his hand out and took my hand in his. He stopped walking and said, "Good night Aella, I'll see you around." Not releasing my hand from his, I knew he was hoping I would stay outside with him for a bit.

"Good night you two. I'll tell Mother you're out here so she doesn't worry. Fina should be home soon too," Aella made a small wave, walked over to the cottage, and disappeared behind the door.

"So would you like to walk or sit?" I gazed at him, not caring which of the two we did.

"How about walk a little, and then sit" he said smiling. The evening was beautiful while the half moon hung over the churning ocean, as if put there for the two of us to enjoy. We walked for only about two minutes down the beach. It was far enough that Mother and Aella couldn't hear our voices, but close enough that we were still in sight of the little Cottage. It was just then I noticed the cottage door blow open, and close, again. A gentle breeze blew past us and I knew my sister would be gone for the rest of the night.

Cody sat down on the beach facing the water and gently pulled me down to sit between his bent legs, also facing the ocean. He slid his arms around my waist and I leaned back into his chest. I could feel his warm breath on the side of my neck. "Did you have fun tonight?" he whispered.

"Oh yes" I sighed, "It has been...and still is wonderful." I was smiling now, though he couldn't see my face. He caught what I meant and took his right hand from my waist, and slowly slid the tops of his fingers down my right arm to my hand. Entwining our fingers with my hand on top, he pulled our hands onto my waist again. This was nice; I had never experienced anything like this in my entire existence.

"So I would like to know more about you, Cody."

As he moved the hair away from my neck with his face, he placed his lips on my neck and asked, "What would you like to know?"

I inhaled deeply and breathed in his inviting cologne. "Well" I began my voice quivered a little. "I already know about where you grew up, where you go to school, where you work, a lot about your sister…Hmm. Thanks to your sister I sound like a regular stalker."

He squeezed me into his chest and we laughed. "Seeing as how Kailey has already filled you in about me, let's talk about you", he breathed into my ear.

"Not so fast, there must be more about you that Kailey hasn't told me", I leaned my head back into his left shoulder. I paused for moment thinking, then whispered, "I know what she hasn't told me. Have you ever been in love?"

His arms went rigid for a moment then relaxed. "Yes, twice", as he placed his lips on my neck again he continued, "First love was for the ocean" my heart fluttered. "The second was a girl," he said so quietly I could barely hear him.

"Is it rude for me to ask why you broke up?" I pressed on with the questions as he continued to hold me. Now his body was rigid but I didn't retract the question.

"Yes, it would be rude …" he seemed to force a chuckle. However, his voice became a little cooler than before. "She and I dated in high school and when she got accepted into the University of Vancouver. Well we decided it best if we gave our relationship a *break,* except…" he took in a long deep breath. "The week before she left for Vancouver, she and her best friend went out in their Sea Kayaks. A storm blew up while they were still out and they didn't come back. They organized searches but," his voice was slow. "Their bodies were washed ashore before anyone had to go looking too far," he finished.

My heart sank, I remembered those girls. I was with them…when they died. They were so young and scared, and though I tired to calm the water for them to get back ashore, they were too far out and I was too late getting there. I knew they would send others to look for them so I made sure to take them to a part of the shoreline where I knew their bodies would be found easily. My heart sank, "I'm sorry Cody and I shouldn't have pressed that way. Please forgive my rudeness." Probably more sorry than he would ever understand.

"It's okay, I've found my peace with it now and if I thought you were really being rude, I wouldn't have told you," he replied softly. I could sense from his tone a gentle smile might be on his face if I were to look. He continued, "But I really didn't intend to talk about this tonight, do you think we could talk about you for awhile?"

I felt the mood lighten. "Sure, what would you like to know?"

I smiled. "How you felt the first day you saw me?"

There was relief in his voice now that it was my turn to talk, as he nuzzled his nose into the side of my neck he took a deep breath.

"Do you want the truth or do you want to hear what would be socially correct for me to say in this situation?" I smiled waiting for his response.

"Well, seeing as how I have been laying it out and hiding nothing you may as well do the same thing," Cody said in a light, throw away tone. "I felt like I was looking into a set of eyes that I had know for my entire existence. I feel so drawn to you. It was like I was looking at someone that could see my soul and I theirs. Like I knew you so well; like we had been together always." My words came faster and faster like the truth of that day had been longing to be heard, and now that it was free to come out, it wasn't going to be stopped mid sentence. "I felt quite overwhelmed and that is why I…ended up where it did. Oh boy, I hope I haven't freaked you out."

He hadn't moved a muscle since I started talking and I couldn't assess the expression on his face as my back was still pressed against his chest. I felt him let his breath out and it sent a shiver down my back. He squeezed his arms around me a little more and said with a huge sigh, "Are you always this honest?" Cody had an air of relief in his voice.

We continued talking until the sun crested the horizon behind us. When the light started dancing off the ocean, for the first time all night I was aware of the time. I felt a breeze brush past my cheek and wondered if it was my sister returning from her evening. "I guess I should get home now," Cody said with a sigh. In one fluid motion Cody stood up, pulling me with him. He turned my body to face his and pulled me in tight. I nuzzled my face in under his chin, partially to avoid his eyes, but mostly cause it felt nice. He held me for a moment and then slid his hand up my arm to meet my face. He stroked my cheek gently, took my chin in his hand, and placed his warm lips on my forehead. I closed my eyes with enjoyment, my heart racing, and for a moment I forgot to be careful. His beautiful warm lips were pressing against mine now. Suddenly, I was pulled out of this wonderful place he and I were sharing, by the sound of Mother: "Naida, Naida are you still out there dear?" She knew I was, but why would she interrupt now? "Yes, Mother", I replied very curtly.

Cody pulled me back close to him after our interruption had split us and his body became rigid, "What the hell, look at the ocean Naida?" Even before I turned, I knew what I would see. The swales were huge; the water was crashing into itself. We both just stood and stared, but I also focused on slowing my heart rate and swimming with whales. Within a couple minutes the ocean became calm. "Wow, the ocean has been acting really odd the last week," Cody said with a deep look of concern on his face. I was careful not to leave my eyes on his for too long.

"Yeah, I've noticed that too," I said.

As he started to back away, a smile parted his lips. "So Naida, this sounds sort of *stupid* but can I call you later."

My eyes went wide with surprise "Ah...No!"

"D-Did you say—No?" he was looking almost deflated now, and hurt at my answer.

I quickly said, "Yes. I said No but I mean...we don't own a phone."
"What? That is the worst rejection I have ever heard anyone getting!" his hurt voice seemed to almost cut me.
"But you're not getting it. We really don't have a phone!" I yelled and ran to him as he was retreating even faster than before. I grabbed his arm and starting trying to pull him back towards the beach, which was rather pointless give his size and strength verses mine.

I suddenly heard Mother again: "Naida! Please." The look in Cody's eyes had changed as he was now focused on the ocean once more. "What is going on?" he asked. I didn't have to look; I knew I needed to calm down.

As I felt my heart rate slow, I tried again, "I'm not kidding about the phone. You can come in and see if you want".

He looked into my eyes and slowly said, "You're serious. Wow, I don't think I can name anyone else without phone." He stood motionless waiting to see if I was going to change my story and when I didn't, a smile broke across his face again. "Okay, so can I send you a smoke signal then?" We both laughed. However, mine was more out of relief that he wasn't still upset. "The new weekend staff are on today and tomorrow, so I should be around. I mean, if you would like to go home and have a nap, I'll be here most of the day." I said.

He pulled me into his firm warm chest once more and whispered in my ear, "I'll be back." He released me and threw me a wink. As he started up the hill from the beach I heard him laughing saying, "No Phone," and shaking his head. I laughed and headed back down to the cottage.

TIDES

"Fina, when did you get back?" I had forgotten all about her staying with Ian until I saw her standing in the Cottage. I closed the door behind me and noticed they had stopped talking. All eyes were on me and I realized that this was the first time I had ever had such an enjoyable evening without have being in the ocean to enjoy it. Fina and Aella went back to what they were doing rather quickly; despite the fact that I knew they had a million questions. Mother took my hand and said, "Come with me Naida, we need a little *Mother daughter talk.*"

"A what?!" I asked, only catching Fina and Aella laughing under their breath before I was pulled out the door.

By the time Mother had finished, I was completely enlightened on the topic of 'the Birds and the Bees' as most people put it. I was left with the feeling that information would have been very helpful *before* last night. However it could have made the tides worse. Only one question stuck in my mind to ask Mother. "Did you know I would feel so strongly for Cody?"

"The connected one's and I thought, if the match was as we had suspected, it would be a good match, a strong match, and a potentially dangerous one at first. It has…exceeded our expectation." She finished surveying my expression. "This is the bond you were hoping for, Naida, we are sure of that now." A smile lightened her intense face, "Are you surprised?"

"Surprised?" I repeated not grasping the question.

"Surprised at how it makes you feel, like you don't need the ocean the same way? That given the choice between him or the ocean, you could see it being a difficult one?" the smile had faded as she searched my face with each question.

I hesitated, looking for words but they wouldn't come. Finally I said, "Mother, could I have some time in the ocean now?"

A warm understanding grin came over her face as she leaned over and hugged me, "Go but don't be gone too long. He will be back today. I honestly don't think he will sleep much."

I smiled, "Mother Terra, sometimes I think you know too much."

She laughed, "Get going." But I didn't need to be told twice.

CHAPTER 7

Deepest Ocean

I swam with my whales and other friends for along time. They had missed my presence in their waters. The freedom to move effortlessly through the water was elating. The water neither warmed me nor cooled me; it always just brought contentment. I could never feel where the water began and I ended, we were just one. But for the first time in my existence, something, or someone, was missing. Mother's questions kept running through my head, bothering me in a way that I was unprepared for. Bothering me mostly because the answers weren't clear, and things had *always* been clear for me. I needed to get back to the cottage; Cody might be waiting for me.

I entered the cottage and glanced at the clock on the wall; only 2:00 pm. Everyone had gone out, I assumed, as the little cottage sat empty, I decided to go out and sit on the beach for a while. Time passed slowly, until I began to hear someone behind me, breathing heavily. It was Cody, and apparently he had decided to jog over.

"Hey Naida" he flashed me a beautiful smile and said, "give me a second". He ran over to the shoreline and peeled off his tight running shirt to reveal his perfectly sculpted torso. He slipped off his shoes and disappeared into the water. He was only in the water for a moment or two when he resurfaced and started walking back to me. I sat silently watching the beads of salt water run from his hair, down his muscular chest to the waistband of his shorts. I stopped there as I could feel my cheeks begin to heat up, my thoughts now being far more imaginative since my talk with Mother.

Then my thoughts switched to a possible problem; what if he held me with the salt water on his skin; what would become of my body? Not wanting to find out, and knowing that he would want to hold me as much as I him, I said, "Let me get you a towel."

He replied immediately, "Sit down, I prefer to dry off this way." He put his shirt on the warm sand and sat down on it. Okay, so I would need to keep him talking until most of the water was gone from him.

"So did you get any sleep after you left here this morning?"

"No not really, how 'bout you?"

"Not a wink. Did you see Kailey this morning?"

He threw his head back and laughed "Yeah, that's maybe another reason why I didn't sleep. *'Cody did you kiss her? Cody did you make another date? Cody? Cody? Cody?'* Agh, little sisters! You know you are in for the third degree on Monday." Thank goodness, he was almost dry 'cause I didn't know how much longer I could sit across from him like this.
"Are you off tomorrow, too?" I said still stalling for a bit more time.
"Yeah, why? What would you like to do tomorrow?" he questioned.
"Hmm, I don't know. Maybe a little more of this." I could see his chest was dry now, so I slid over beside him and leaned into his face with mine. As I got close, he reached his hand up to hold my chin as gently as he had the night before. His kiss was so soft and warm. I could have stayed right there for the rest of the day. This time I remembered to

control the tides in my head while we kissed. I ran my hand up his back and felt the warm, wet touch of his skin. Wet…No!! No, No, not wet! But if anyone knew what water felt like, it was me. I left my hand around his back, and as we pulled apart I glanced down at my other hand. It was still in the same physical state as before, so just to be sure I launched myself into his lap and threw my arms around him. Now I could look at my other hand over his shoulder. It was fine; I would need to talk to Mother about this later. I really didn't know all the rules to my transformation.

"I thought that you might like to go for a walk. I could show you my house and you could stay for dinner if you would like." He finished a little more hesitantly.

"That sounds great. Let me get my sweater and shoes from the cottage." I jumped up and ran over to the cottage. I was feeling pretty proud of myself for keeping the waters calm. I pushed the door to the cottage open and realized he was right behind me. "Come on in." I told him as I could feel his hand on the small of my back, which sent a shiver up my spine.

"I love this place, it's so rustic and warm. How long have you been here?" his eyes were wide taking in all our things.

"Only a few months. We like it though," I turned quickly to face him, with only a few inches between our noses "You're checking to make sure I really don't have a phone aren't you? You know you were."

He scooped me up in his arms and pulled me close to his body. His chest was still bare and warm from the sun. The top of my head only came up to his eyes, so when he held me like this I could nuzzle into his neck with my face and breathe in the aroma of his cologne.

He breathed a deep sigh, "We should go. Grab your sweater." As he released me, I could see a struggled look on his face, while he pulled on his shirt.

"Sure but are you okay?" I was concerned.

"Yeah, better then okay," his wonderful smile returned to his face.

"Oh...Okay."

We started up the hill just outside the cottage, when I felt a gentle breeze go past my head. As I looked back towards the cottage Aella was waving good-bye to me while holing a towel around herself. I threw her a smile with a wink, and continued along by Cody's side. Funny; we had spent so much time together for so many years that I could always tell when she was near. I still hadn't had a chance to talk to her since the party; I wonder how much she knew.

We walked for about 20 minutes until we came to an old equisitely classic looking home. As we walked up the lane he said, "What do you think?"

"It's beautiful...Wow! This is your place, have you lived here long?"

"Yeah, all my life." as his pulled me into his body he turned me so my back was next to his chest, and we faced a stunning view of a bay.
"That is Mahone Bay. I think that is one of the reasons why I love this place so much. That view is like an old friend to me. Come on, I'll take you inside." But before he loosened his arms, he bent his head down to kiss my neck. I let out a reassuring sigh.

"This is beautiful, Cody. How old is this home?" I said as I admired the craftsmanship of the chair rails and wainscoting.

"It was built in the 1700's by my great, great, great grandfather. Actually, I may be off by a "great" or two, but you get the idea. One of them lost the house in a poker game, but my grandfather bought it back and handed it on to my dad. Pretty cool, eh." He smiled, looking very proud of his home, not in an arrogant way, just pleased. He picked up my hand and led me around his house, pointing out all of its historical features.

"Your home is beautiful," I said, truly impressed.

"No, you're beautiful; the house is historical," and he brushed the tips of his fingers across my cheek and down my neck. With the other hand he reached around my back and pulled me in close to him. My heart began to race and my face flushed, but I still kept control of my mind. I think I had found the balance to this entire holding stuff; just don't lose control. Then his hand, by my neck, slid down my arm to the middle of my back. He put his face into my neck and I could feel his breath warm me. He turned his face and our lips were touching, and then as if caressing my lips with his, he began kissing me. I could feel my temperature rise as if I had just sat on a bonfire. His pulse was quick as he brought his hand down to my waist.

Suddenly a voice called "Cody, are you home?" We both froze.

As Cody pulled his face away from mine he cleared his throat and called back.

"Yes, Mom we'll be right down." He smiled at me, both of us feeling like we had just had a bucket of cold water thrown on us. "You'll love my Mom. She makes the best pan-fried halibut around."

"Well, I'm not loving her too much right now," a little disappointed with the interruption. "But I'm sure I will," I raised only one side of my mouth in a crooked smile.

She's making fish for dinner, I thought to myself. What if I swam with this little guy? I swim with halibut quite often. Oh, how was I going to handle this one?

He caught my hand in his and I followed him downstairs.

"Mom this is Naida, the girl I was telling you about, and that Kailey works with." He was beaming at his mom as he introduced us.

"Hello Naida, I'm Emily. I'm so glad to finally meet you. Between Kailey and Cody, I think I know you better then my neighbors." She smiled as Cody shot her a glare.

"Oh Cody, come on. She must know she's the only thing you've talked about for the last week." She walked by him and ruffled his hair.

Sounding totally mortified, he said, "Well Mom, she does now". He wasn't too mad though, because the next minute he was back to normal, "Hey, what time is dinner Mom? I want to show Naida the backyard."

"4:30. Your dad will be home soon from Kayaking. He promised to take me out to a movie, and I thought we would eat first. Your sister is staying at Sue's house tonight." She said pulling some meat out of the fridge. "Do you like hamburgers, Naida?"

"Oh yes that would be wonderful. Thank you, Emily." I smiled in relief.

"Okay, well go on. I'll call you when it's ready," she said smiling.

"Great, thanks Mom," Cody pulled my hand and we ducked out the kitchen door to the backyard. We walked across the grass and came to this huge tree in the yard. About 10 feet up was the cutest little house.

"My dad and I built this tree house about 15 years ago, and it's still rock solid." He started climbing the ladder attached to the tree, "Come on".

"This is so…cute," I replied with a giggle once I was in. I looked around at all the marks and things on the walls. There wasn't enough room for me to stand up so I sat cross-legged on the floor of the tree house. I don't think Cody could even sit up properly, so instead he lay down and put his head in my lap.

"This is wonderful. You and your dad built this," I said appraising their workmanship. "Hey, what does your dad do…for a living, I mean?"

"Oh he works at Dalhousie University. He is a Professor of Marine Conservation." He sounded very proud of his dad.

"Wow, I'm impressed. Hey, would you take me there sometime. I would love to see the University." I was beginning to understand the connection I had to Cody more and more, and it just made me feel more attracted to him.

"I would love that, Naida." His smile broke his lips apart.

We talked for a little while longer until we heard Emily calling for us.

"Dinner's ready, kids."

"Coming" Cody called as he helped me down the ladder. He let his hand slide over my butt as he turned up the edge of his mouth, "Oops, sorry," not meaning a word of it.

Once inside, Cody introduced me to his Dad "Naida, this is my Dad". He stuck out his hand. As I shook it he said, "You can call me Paul, and it is very nice to meet you." He shot an approving glance at Cody as we sat down at the table. Dinner and the conversation were wonderful, but before too long Emily and Paul were clearing the dishes getting ready to go out to the movie.

"Don't be too late tonight Cody. You look dead tired and you don't want to get too far behind on your sleep. Here are the keys to my car. You make sure you get Naida home safely," as she tossed him a set of keys.

"Good Night Mr. and Mrs. Angel. Enjoy the movie, and thank you for dinner," I said as they collected their things to go.

"Oh well, thank you for joining us. It was very nice to meet you, and you're welcome back anytime. Good night." Emily finished and turned to leave.

"Good Night kids, and your Mom's right Cody, not too late tonight." Paul reinforced his wife's request.

"Good Night," Cody answered.

He did look really tired, and I knew that I could use a little dip in the ocean.

"Would you like me take you home soon, or …" we both smiled at each other.

"Home would probably wise, Cody. You do look pretty tired." I smiled and moved my hand across his chest. "Why don't you drive me home and we can sit on the beach until sunset, then you can come home and climb into bed."

He flashed a very sly smile as though he were elaborating on my suggestion in his head. Whatever it is was in his smile, it made me turn eight shades of red.

"Well, we know where your intentions lay," I said as I pulled him out to his Mom's car. As I looked back at him, he was making this pouty face at me.

Before I could open the door though, he put his arms around my waist, and as he pulled me to his body he said, "Are you sure you want to go, 'cause the offer is only good for, I don't know, maybe 100 more years." He smiled and kissed me on the forehead while he opened my door.

"Sounds like I have some time then," I smiled as I slide into the car.

"Yup, as much as you want or need." He said, "I don't think I'll be going too far from your side," as he shut my door.

Back on my beach the waves came in and out. I could feel I would need to be with them soon. I hadn't stored enough energy to last very long, so Cody and I sat until sunset. I nestled between his legs like I had the night before. I felt the touch of his forehead on my shoulder and the rhythmic sound of his breathing, and knew he had been falling asleep. I enjoyed the sound of his breathing for a while before I thought, I better get him up so he could get home for a proper sleep. He argued for a minute, and then agreed as he yawned in my ear.

"Have a good sleep tonight, Cody. I'll dream of you so I won't miss you so much," I smiled though the thought of not being with him pained me. "Please drive carefully".

"I will, I have a lot to live for! I will see you tomorrow. Okay?" he shot me that beautiful smile and started up the hill.

"Oh wait," he turned back and was beside me before I knew what he had said. "I need something before I leave." And with that he scooped me up in his arms and gently put his lips on mine. With the intensity of his kiss increasing every moment, he finally pulled back. His breathing was accelerated and hard now. 'That will keep me awake until I'm home," he smiled.

"Glad I could help, I'll see you tomorrow," I replied, smiling back at him.
When he was over the top of the hill, I turned back to the water and prepared to get in over by the small gathering of trees. As I dove in my thoughts were filled only of Cody. My love for Cody was becoming as deep as my love for my ocean. I knew this was fast, but it was so natural that it didn't seem to matter how fast it went.

The whale family that I often swam with seemed to be waiting for me about 3 kilometers out. When I communicate with the ocean life, it is not done by sound as it is on land. We communicate by thought so distance is less of a problem when communicating at longer ranges. I almost swam right by the family, when three of the larger whales caught my attention. I was still deeply in thoughts of Cody.

"Naida?" the largest one said. "Is that you?" wondering if I was with them or not.

"Yes, how are you?" I was picking up on the thought of the others now, also. Something seemed to be wrong. Something *was* terribly wrong judging by the panic I sensed in their thoughts. "What is it, what has happened?"

"Follow us," the largest said gravely.

We swan for about 20 more kilometers when we came to it. A huge net had been dragged some distance and caught up all the ocean life in its path. Deep in the netting, amongst all the creatures' fear and confusion, I sensed something more. The great whale that I followed to this site was communicating to another caught in the netting. "She is here now, if anyone can help your brother, she can."

"He is your brother?" I asked, horrified.

"Yes. It happened less than an hour ago, and we were hoping you would be back soon enough to help. Is there anything you can do to help him?" she said hopefully.

"Let me circle and see if there is a way out. Stay here and I will be back." The net was still on the move, scooping up more and more ocean life. It was breaking my heart to see this, and I would need to act fast if I was going to help any of them. I circled twice to be sure, and returned to the whale family in the back, following the net.

"The big trawler boats are still filling the net, so tell your brother to swim towards the direction of the pull as hard and fast as he can. When he is free of the other fish, tell him he needs to swim down as deeply as he can go. This net doesn't go as deep as most, so he will be able to watch it pass him from underneath, and then he can rejoin you. He must hurry, though. I don't know how long they will pull the net for." I would have loved to ask him to take as many fish with him, but chances of them following a killer whale were slim.

When he started to swim, you could see the tension on the netting change, so we knew he would need to swim fast now. We followed the net quietly, waiting, letting their brother focus on what he needed to do. Finally, we heard his song from far below us; the giant whale I had followed before, returned his song. He was free, and back up with his family in moments. The net had damaged his skin, but he was free.

I watched the net continue on its way, with many fish already dead and others that would die, and that humans wouldn't use. And this wasn't the worst of it; some nets did far more damage to my under water world. I needed this to stop. It was killing me, and the human's didn't seem to understand it would eventually kill them too.

The Whale family thanked me and went to the surface for a bit. I said good-bye with a heavy heart. While I was up enjoying myself with Cody, what was I not protecting in my ocean? I wish I could stop every ship from going out into my ocean while I was human. Maybe I could, perhaps if I stayed very angry all the time. The ocean would be too rough for them to go out on. However, I knew that wouldn't solve anything. I needed to help the humans. I needed to help Cody.

I swam for the rest of the night, storing my energy for my time on land. I seemed to have so much weighing on me now, however, I knew it was time. I felt that if I tried to have secrets or hide things from Cody, it would be moving in the wrong direction for my end goal. It also seemed pointless. He needed to love me for all that I am, not just what he thinks he knows. Because time was ticking for my ocean and I, it had to be soon. I decided I would find a way tomorrow. Cody needed to know.

When I returned to the shore, Mother was waiting for me.

"You okay?" she asked with deep concern.

"Yes, Mother, but it is getting..." I sighed and paused as I continued pulling on the rest of my clothes, "...complicated."

"How so Naida, has something changed?" Mother asked surveying my face.

"I suppose not, just what if when I reveal *myself* to Cody for who I am, I lose him? I don't want to lose him, Mother! He brings me hope and a depth of love that I have only felt for one other, and that one other is so connected to me, and contains so many lives within it." I said slowly and sadly.

"He feels strongly for the ocean too Naida, you share that. It is very important that you explain it in a way that he can totally understand *what* you are. And that the love he feels for the ocean is the same love he feels for you, though it can be expressed with you differently. But when your eyes meet, Naida, he sees who and what you are. But because he has never seen this before, it's like he can bring it into focus. It's there, and I know you know it is. No matter how you tell him, he will struggle with the concept of it, just be thorough. Don't leave any room for him to think it some kind of magic trick." She spoke in a low comforting voice. "He is the one; we are sure of that."

"Thank you Mother". I smiled only out of courtesy, not feeling much joy at all. "Naida, I know you feel that you are needed in the ocean to protect it's life more than up here doing what we are doing, but I assure you that you are doing more good up here in the long run. For us and all of humanity, the long run is what is important. Do you understand what I mean?" she asked as we walked up the beach together.

"Yes", I said. A tear filled the corner of my eye and rolled down my cheek as I remembered the net with all the ocean life, and death, within it.

"I was with the connected ones yesterday while your sisters spent time with their energy sources. They too are very proud of you and your bravery." She smiled and hugged me.

"Mother, who are these connected ones and why do I not see them?" I inquired.

"Well, for one thing, you don't need to see them right now, but they exist on the same plane as the one I visit to contact you when you are in the ocean, or when any of you are with your source. They have been on these shores for many years and they help to protect nature in many ways. The humans refer to them as spirits; spirits of the Mi'kmaq tribe. The Native people have taken many walks with me, and they understand us in ways many people do not grasp. They have looked to me for answers, and I to them. I have several generations of chiefs that I look to for their wisdom on that plane. Does that help?" she finished with a half smile turning up in one corner of her mouth.

"Yes, thank you!" I said, now remembering another question I had almost forgotten to ask Mother. "Yesterday after Cody had been in the water, I touched some water on his back, and it didn't do anything to me. Why is that?"

"Good question", she began with a chuckle and a smile. "It was no longer connected to the main energy source. When you change, you change because the source feels you enter the water, as all the life in the ocean feels you enter. They are all aware of your presence or lack of presence. So one drop of disconnected ocean water has no effect, no more than a bucket of ocean water would, if you were standing well away from the ocean. As long as the droplets don't connect back to the source, you can stay in your physical form. But…that doesn't mean to say you can't control salt water or ocean water when it is not connected to the source. When you connect with it, you become its source, and it then responds to your emotions. When the salt water senses a change in your emotions, it reacts. Smaller amounts of the water will react faster than the ocean does to you." Mother smiled and then called out, "We are over here, girls."

My sisters; I haven't seen them in a bit, and realized at the sight of them that I had missed them. Aella ran over and threw her arms around me. Fina flashed me a smile. "We need to talk," Aella began, and Fina agreed. They grilled me for what seemed like hours on the beach about Cody and all that had happened with him. I was actually happy to tell them because I knew they could relate more than anyone else would be able to. Fina seemed to have a special understanding. Aella just understood because of how well she knew me.

"Will you see him today?" Aella asked. But before she could finish her question, a handsome, dark haired 20 year old male appeared, coming towards us down the hillside. A smile consumed my face, and both Aella and Fina whipped their heads around in his direction. The two of them jumped up from where we had been sitting and talking.

"I think we have many things we need to do that can't wait, don't you Aella?" Fina said smiling at the two of us.

"Yes, I'm right behind you. Bye." Aella threw me a wink and Fina laughed.

"Bye, I'll see you later. Back to work tomorrow," I replied.
I watched them smile at Cody as they passed each other. My sisters made their way to the cottage, and Cody to me.

CHAPTER 8

Exposed

"I brought you coffee but I realized half way here that I don't even know if you drink it," he said thoughtfully, with a beautiful smile lighting up his face.

As I stood up I said "Honestly…I've never tried it." I wrinkled my nose and squinted my eyes in embarrassment. "You've never tried coffee?" he sounded surprised.

I took both coffees out of his hands and pushed the cups into the sand so they wouldn't fall over. As I stood up; he was on to what I was about to do, before I could begin. He slipped both his arms around my waist and pulled me onto his warm firm chest. I gazed into his eyes, enjoying his soul, all the while remembering to control the ocean behind me. I allowed him to stare back into mine, hoping the longer he looked, the better he could focus. He bent his head down to place his lips on mine. His mouth had a funny taste almost bitter, but it wasn't that bad, so I enjoyed the kiss. As we broke apart he took my chin in his hand and leaned into my ear. With his breath warming my neck he said, "You don't have to drink the coffee. In fact I like this much better." He leaned back and looked into my eyes again, pulling back the corner of his mouth in a half-devilish smile. Then his expression changed. His eyes still on mine, he said, "Are you okay?"

Maybe he was starting to focus but just didn't know what it was he was seeing. "I'm fine. I'm so happy you're here."

How would I tell him?

I bent down to pick up the coffees. As I stood up, I handed him the one that looked as though he had been drinking out of already. I put the other cup to my lips and took a sip. "Bitter" I said with a smile. "Come on, I want you to meet my *Moth*...Mom." I corrected myself.

Mother was hanging some clothes on a small line outside, "Mom I want you to met Cody."

She turned with a smile. She put out her hand, but not in a handshake sort of way, more like a palm reader with her hand palm face up. Cody placed his right hand in hers and she placed her other hand on top. As she cupped his hand in hers, she said with great depth and conviction in her voice, "It is wonderful to meet you. Naida has spoken so highly of you."

Cody's voice seemed to break from the intensity of Mother's welcome. "Thank you Mrs. Terra. I really enjoy her company." He finished with a smile.

"Please Cody, call me Anna. Mrs. Terra is far too formal," she said in a much lighter tone.

"Thank you...Anna" he stumbled slightly.

"What are you kids up to today, or do you know yet?" Mother laughed.

"Nope but I'm sure we will come up with something." I smiled at Cody "See you later Mom".

"Bye kids," said replied and Cody waved.

We started up the hill. Cody finished his coffee and said, "What do you want to do today?"

As I caught sight of the little Prius waiting for us on the side of the road, I replied, "Hum, you decide?" I thought he might have already had something in mind, so I was just going to let him go with it. My biggest concern was how to reveal my secret, without sending him packing. So where ever we ended up would likely be fine. I was winging it, anyway.

"Great". His eyes lit up, "Lets go". He opened the door for me and watched me get in. After he closed the door he rounded the car, got in and said, "I hope you don't mind, but I have a little spot up the coast I'd like to share with you." He smiled as he started the car.

We drove for 30 or 40 minutes up the coast. We turned down a road and then Cody parked the Prius. He grabbed a knapsack from the back seat and jumped out of the car. I got out, and quickly joined him. He put his arm around me and glided me down a path. Despite the trees on either side of us, I could still feel my ocean not far away. Finally, we came out of the trees and there it was, waiting for us. My ocean looked so beautiful from here. We walked along the deserted beach talking and laughing. Cody finally stopped, took out a blanket from his knapsack, and laid it out on the sand.

"Would you like something to drink? I noticed the coffee went over like a lead balloon," he said laughing.

We drank water, ate and laughed and talked into the late afternoon. He stood and said, "You want to go in?" with a cheerful smile beaming from his face.

It was time; I had to be careful now, no doubt, no tricks.

"Cody would you sit back down for a minute, and yes I would like to swim with you. But I need to talk to you first." I started tentatively.

"Okay. You look so serious. It's just a swim."

"No, I need to share something with you. But I am terrified of how it will make you feel."

"You're not a guy, or ever were a guy, are you?" his eyes were wide and joking.

"No, would you be serious and just listen, please. I am very connected to the ocean. I mean in ways that regular people aren't. The water affects me as much as I can affect the water." I took his hand in mine "Please promise me that you won't freak out. It would hurt me deeply if I lost you now."

"Whatever it is, I'm sure I can deal with it Naida. Give me some credit." He smiled.

"Okay," I said as I ducked behind a sign that had been posted on the beach. I was perfectly fine with Cody seeing me naked, but I sensed it might embarrass him, so I disrobed behind the sign. I didn't know why humans had this thing with their bodies. They were beautiful. Such a wonderful creation to be appreciated; never hidden or ashamed of. But one hurdle at a time. Once he sees my body hit the water I will disappear, and I will have to do this carefully, in order for him to understand.

"Are you watching the sign?" I yelled out.

"Yes my eyes are on the sign, your ankles and feet. That is all I can see." A little chuckle slipped out.

I ran out straight into the water. By the time I was up to where my knees should have been, the rest of my body was completely dissolved. He ran to the shoreline yelling my name, but I couldn't answer him. Well at least not until his feet were in the water, connecting him, so I could talk to him through his mind.

The sound of panic grew stronger in his calls, "Naida, Naida where are you? I can't see you." He still wasn't touching the water and the concern was growing in his voice. His head moved side to side, his eyes moving fast, scanning the water, but clearly not finding me. I couldn't stand it any longer, so I came out right in front of him and my physical body was back. His jaw dropped, and I wasn't sure what was more of a shock, the fact that I had just materialized right in front of his eyes, or the fact that I was naked. Talk about women that play mind games; this one could go down as a world record!

"I'm sorry, I didn't know how to put it into words, so I thought it would be better to show you." I said very apologetically.

"What the...I...I don't understand". Cody started to pace back and forth. Then he stopped, looked at me, and was clearly searching for words but when nothing came out, he went back to pacing."
"Did you just disappear, Naida?"

But before I could answer, he pressed his fingertips into his eyes as if to clear them of something that was irritating them. Blinking his eyes twice more, he stopped pacing again and just stared.

I stood, quiet and still, waiting for it to finish sinking in.

"Okay let's get this straight I'm not scared but totally confused." As he took a couple deep breaths he said, "Make me understand, please." He finished slowly, still looking at me, dumb struck, but much calmer now.

"Okay." I reached over and pulled off his shirt, throwing it onto the beach behind him. "Could you pick me up, please," I asked in a tiny voice.

I sensed this was very difficult for him, so I added, "I trust you to be a gentleman, you know." I finished with a smile.

As he scooped me up with one arm under my knees and the other around my back he smiled back, at me with one eyebrow raised, "A trust that I may not be deserving of".

I put my arms around his neck and asked him to start walking into the water. My feet dangled close to the water. I put my hands on either side of his face and I placed my lips on his while he continued to walk forward into the water. My feet touched first, and I knew he was aware of the full affect now, as I dissolved away from his body into the water again. He just stood there; not a sound from his lips.

But this time he was in the water and connected. I sent a thought to his mind. "I'm still right here with you. I'm just part of the water."

"How did you do that?" His voice came softly now, but aloud.

"This is how I communicate in the water with all creatures, you included," I replied, very relieved to see he wasn't running for the car…at least not yet.

"Can you come out now?" he said with a very straight face.

"Sure. But why?" I asked in his thought
"Because my girlfriend's beautiful body is much easier to look at while I try to figure this out. Well, okay maybe distracting, but better that than this." He said with a slight smile.

Within a second I was up on the beach again, and he walked towards me. He placed a hand on my shoulder as if waiting to see if I would disappear again.

I smiled, "I'm still here.'

"I can see that. My head is swimming." He reached over to pull me close to him, the warmth of his chest against mine. He kissed my forehead gently, took a very deep breath and said, "I think you should put some clothes on so I can concentrate on more than just your body." He smiled and let me slip away to get my clothes. He returned to the blanket on the beach. He sat there waiting patiently for me to return.

As I sat down he said, "I have so many questions, and I don't know where to begin."

I moved closer to him and asked him one. "I need to know something before you start with your questions." I paused for a moment. It was something I should have asked before I revealed myself to him, but I couldn't change that now. "Do you love me as much as I love you?"

He didn't even hesitate "Yes, and that I am very sure of." His look of sincerity was unwavering.

"Then I will answer all that you would like to know," I replied, feeling extremely relieved.

We talked for hours and hours; his questions were very intuitive. Finally, he looked more tired than overwhelmed, so I suggested we head back and let him sleep on the next round of questions. He agreed, and we packed up.

As he drove home he held my hand. We sat in silence for the first time since his jaw had almost fallen off by the ocean. I knew he was just processing the day's events in his head, and I would have expected nothing less. He parked the car at the side of the road and walked me to the cottage.

Finally I broke the silence: "I know this may sound a little *stupid* right now but can we keep this between us?" I used some of his own words, in reference to the phone the day before.

"No," he replied with a sly little grin.

"What?" I replied, looking shocked.

"No, Naida I want the entire world to know I'm in love with you!" he finished bending his neck to kiss me. "As for the other thing, my lips are sealed".

"Good…oh, will I see you tomorrow?" I said hopefully.

"Oh yes, you will see me tomorrow for sure. Are you going home or into the cottage?" he asked now enjoying the secret, which wasn't a secret, with him, anymore.

I cocked my head to the side and replied with a smile, "Home."

He kissed me on the lips and said, "Be safe tonight, for me. I still can't quite get my head around you swimming with killer whales and all."

I laughed, humoring his request. "Okay, I'll be careful for you." Still laughing, I left him and headed for the cluster of trees.

Quiet aware that he hadn't moved from the spot at which I left him, I undressed behind the trees and dove in. I waited to watch him turn and go back up the hill. As I swam out, I wondered what he was thinking about.

CHAPTER 9

Jealousy

The next morning Aella, Fina, and I all got ready for work. It felt like I had been away for so long and so much had happened in such a short period of time. However it had only been two days off work. The walk was nice; Fina filled me in on her time with Ian. It sounded like they were just having some fun, which suited Fina just fine, she told us.

We got to work on time and went down to the staff room to meet up with everyone. Kailey and Mary were waiting for Aella and I. Fina put her things away and took off up to the lounge. Kailey's smile couldn't have been any bigger; I thought she would explode if we didn't quickly get to the first room with our trolley where she could talk freely.

We entered the room and she pounced, like a tiger upon its prey.

"What have you done with my brother?" she began, "I have never seen him like this. He's even being nice to me!" she added with a chuckle. "I knew you guys would hit it off, didn't I? I should be a matchmaker; just pair people up for a living. That would be good. Anyway, you look happier than I've seen you look…ever!" she breathed quickly.

"Thanks Kailey, I feel wonderful," I said, elated.

We worked pretty hard for most of the day. During lunch in the staffroom, I saw some girls pointing at me and talking. I looked at Kailey, "What is that all about?"

"They're jealous that you and my brother have hit it off so well. Don't worry though, they'll get over it." Kailey finished, still beaming at me every time we talked. I guess she approved of me with her brother.

Kailey and I were just finishing up in the last room on our list. I was cleaning the bathroom while she finished up the beds. I was bent over cleaning the sides of the tub, when I heard from the doorway, "Now the view yesterday on the beach was much better, but this one's pretty good too." My heart raced at the sound of his voice.

"Cody", I hadn't scared him off yesterday! He slipped his arms around my waist and pulled me to his chest, and in a low voice he said, "How was your swim last night?"

"Wonderful, the only way it would have been better was if you had been with me," I replied in a whisper.

Still in a hushed voice he said, "I stayed to watch you get in the water last night. Your body against the moon…was stunning" his breathing was a little heavier now.

Kailey's voice came from the other room, "Okay, I don't mean to be pushy but we need to get out of the room. Naida, are you almost done?"

"Yup," as I finished spraying down the tub.

"Great, why don't you guys take the garbage to the garbage room, and I will return the trolley," Kailey offered.

"Sounds like a plan to me," Cody said as he scooped up the garbage in one hand. He waited until we were in the staff corridor before he reached for my hand.

We put the garbage away, and just before we left the corridor I stopped and turned to him, "Are you sure you're okay with everything?" not wanting to be to specific, in case anyone were to walk in.

He gently pushed my back against the wall and put his hands upon the wall on either side of my head. "I have never be so…okay with something as I am with this. It's like we were made for each other, or maybe I was made for you. Whatever the case, I can't stop thinking about you and it drove me nuts not being with you today."

My smile must have looked pretty silly, but I didn't care. We were made for each other. "Do you have your parents' car today?" I asked now beginning to make some plans in my head.

"Yup, but I'm not off until two in the morning," he said in a gloomy tone.
"And if I needed sleep, that might sound like a bad thing, but I don't. I can just make sure I'm out of the water by then," I said with a sneaky smile.
"Of course…hmm. But do me a favor," he said as he raised one eyebrow, "Don't rush, cause I wouldn't want to miss the *show*!"

I hit his arm in a playful way, and rolled my eyes at him, "Come on."
We met Kailey and Aella in the staffroom. Some of the other girls stared at Cody, hopeful that they might catch his eye.

As we went to leave, he gently put his hand on the small of my back to guide me out of the staffroom. I'm not sure that he didn't do it as a subtle gesture to indicate that we were, in fact, together for the benefit of the other hopeful female eyes, watching and waiting to see if the rumors were true.

Cody walked us upstairs to the front of the Beach Club where Fina was waiting. Fina was laughing to herself about something; I was sure she would fill us in on the way home. Cody walked us all down the stairs and then grabbed my hand and stopped.

"Go ahead, I'll catch up in a minute," I flashed a smile and Kailey, Aella, and Fina all understood my meaning and continued walking.

"So I'll see you tonight then, on the beach?" he was more confirming than asking.

"Yup, I'll be sure to be out in time," I smiled and blushed a little.
He raised his eyebrow and winked with the other eye, "Well, at least I will have that to look forward to tonight." He gave me a quick yet gentle kiss, and retreated up the stairs.

I ran to catch up to the girls but they were walking pretty slowly so they hadn't gotten too far. They were talking about something that Janie had told Aella about Cody.

"She said that Cody was a player, and would be on to his next victim in no time," Aella said in a mimicking voice.

Kailey's head spun around to Aella, and had she possessed claws, I think they would have been out. "That witch! She is so jealous right now...Agh! She has been crushing on my brother for the last 2 years, at least. One night last year, during one of Ian's bonfires, Cody had to make it very clear to her that he wasn't interested. She had been coming on to him so strongly. Naida, promise me you won't listen to that girl."

I put my arm around Kailey's shoulder and said, "I promise, as long as *you* promise to calm down." I smiled at Kailey and her face returned to its former cheery state, before Janie was mentioned.

We came to the bottom of the long Beach Club entrance. Kailey turned right, while the rest of us turned left to go home. The three of us said good-bye to Kailey and kept walking.

We chatted for a bit and then I remembered something. "Hey, Fina, what were you laughing at in front of the Beach Club when we picked you up?"

"Oh yeah, I almost forgot. Just before you got there, this woman pulled up in a very sleek looking car with two friends. You could tell they thought they are all that, and more. I was laughing because I don't think there was much *original hardware* left on any one of them." Fina laughed again.

"What do you mean Fina, when you say *original hardware*?" I was lost, Fina and Aella knew so much more about this stuff than I did. They had been able to observe for so much longer than I.

Aella cut in and decided to answer this one. I was relieved of that, 'cause sometimes Fina could answer me in a way that made me fell like I should have known the answer. "Some women," Aella began, "Men too, but not as much, decide they don't like the way they were created. They may not like their hair colour, the way their nose spreads out at the end, their tummies are too lumpy or their boobs are too little. So they change it with surgery, or different hair colour dyes. Can you imagine letting someone cut your skin so they can break bones and re-shape things so you look prettier? Yuck! There's this one surgery that they add a saline filled sack under the skin of your breast just to make them bigger. No other creature on the planet does this. I wish humans could understand how beautiful they are, and how it's the differences that make them beautiful and unique." Aella finished, looking quite sad.

"Really, well that answers my question as to why Sara at the front desk has purple lines through her hair. But what is saline?" I inquired, still a little puzzled.

Fina piped up quickly, I guess she was a little disappointed when *she* didn't get to fill me in on the first question. "Oh you would love that Naida. Saline is salt water! Yup! They put a sack full of salt water under their skin. And let me tell you; this woman had half the ocean in her chest!" We all laughed a little, though it was really quite sad that this woman felt she needed that to feel good about herself. Maybe no one had ever told her how beautiful she was, or how much they loved her. I don't think I would ever understand it, so it was best just to leave it alone. *Half the ocean*, I thought to myself.

We got home in good time. I told Mother I would be out until around 1:30 A.M. but that if she saw Cody sooner, could she please contact me. She agreed, and wished me an enjoyable evening. I wasn't sure which part of my evening she was stressing to be enjoyable, but I assumed it was both.

Aella decided she would join me for part of the evening. I thought the way she transformed into wind was amazing. She was ready before me, and as I watched her beckon the wind to come for her, it responded to her request swiftly. It scooped her up as if she were weightless, and dissolved her as if she were sand into the wind, and then gone. I dove into the waves and within moments we glided effortlessly, Aella in the wind, and I in the water.

"Do you miss your source during the day?" I questioned Aella, after a few minutes of silence.

Aella's tone was light, "I don't miss it that much. It's always so close. It's like I know if I need a little pick me up, I just have to go outside for a little fresh air, as Mary calls it. Not that she knows what I'm doing, but I don't have to transform, to enjoy my source. Obviously, it's much faster for me to collect my energy in this form, but a summer breeze on my physical body's face can always help my mood." She ended with a laugh.

"How do you do it, I mean, not transforming every time you're outside and there is a little gust of wind?" I pressed a little more.

"Focus and practice. It's resisting your natural desire, and it's not easy. Have you not tried it yet?" she sounded surprised at the thought that I hadn't.

"No, I hadn't even thought of it to be honest. Do you think I can?" I asked.

"Sure, and maybe now with Cody in your life, it will be easier. See you have to really want to stay in that form for it to work. It's just a mind thing, I guess."

I liked this; I liked having Aella with me to talk to. She was so calm and understanding of my lack of experience in my new skin. It made me feel like Cody's world seemed closer to me; like it wasn't all a dream. Particularly in the last couple days, I would get out in the ocean by myself and start to wonder if Cody and that life was real, but Aella was living it with me, and that in itself was just reassuring.

"It's a nice night tonight" I said noting of how peaceful everything was.

"Yes, you and your waters are quite calm," she snickered.

"So are you and your winds," we both laughed together when I heard Mother

"Naida. He'll be here soon, I hope you're not too far out."

"Oh my gosh, Aella. I will see you at the cottage later. Love you, and thanks for the talk tonight."

As I changed my direction to head back, she said, giggling at my reaction, "Love you too, see you later," and we were gone our separate ways.

CHAPTER 10

Competition

    Mother had made sure I was back in enough time to get out of the water and dressed before Cody's beautiful, strong, yet comforting silhouette appeared on the hill. I walked towards him, meeting him half way between the hill and the ocean. The warmth of his greeting was not unexpected or unwelcomed. It was nice to be in his arms again. I felt like a piece of me was put back in place every time he was with me. The touch of his skin on mine, whether it was a passionate kiss or just holding my hand; it all felt so natural now, so right.

"How was your evening in the water tonight?" he asked as we stood face to face with his forehead touching mine.

"It was wonderful, but the time almost slipped away on me. I wish I could share my nights in the water with you. You'd love it." I smiled looking into his eyes.

    He smiled and moved his lips onto mine. As he did, he inhaled as if to take in as much of me as possible. "I love this," he said as he smiled and led me down the beach.

"Hey Cody, I was wondering if you would help me with something?" I began.

"Sure what is it?"

"I want to see if I can overcome my natural desire. What I mean to say is that I need to learn to control myself, so that when I'm touching my source I don't just dissolve into it."

"Okay, but how can I help with that?"

"My pull to be with you is growing as strong as my desire to be with my source. What I thought is, if you could hold me while I touched the water, I could try to overcome the water's pull with my desire to stay with you." I blushed a little with the last part of the sentence.

A smile broke over Cody's mouth "This sounds fun to me...as long as none of your friends come to encourage you. The last thing I need is for a killer whale to come and help you get out to *your source*," he finished, frowning at me a little.

"They won't; even when they need me, they have a certain distance at which they will wait for me." I smiled back to his frown.

"Well, that's comforting."

"Yup, I guess I should buy a bathing suit"

"Nope."

"Yes, I should, 'cause you will need to stay focused, but not *that* focused," I laughed at him.

We stopped walking and sat down on the cool sand. "How was your night tonight?" I had almost forgot to ask.

"Oh. It was…fine," he replied, quiet hesitantly.

"Fine? That sounds exciting," I said laughing a little "but you don't sound too sure of yourself."

"Oh it was nothing. Just some drunk guests, you know," as he rolled his eyes. "Nothing. I haven't had to handle before. Hey, did you hear that Ian is going to do another staff bonfire this weekend? I bet you and Kailey could go together again, and I could meet you out there after work." He finished, sounding so excited now.

"Sure, last Friday night was fun, I would love to do that again."

The rest of the week zipped by. Cody visited me every night after work and we talked about the ocean, his schooling, and how great things were in general. We decided to wait for the weekend to try my 'swimming lessons', as we called them, when anyone was around to hear.

Friday came before we knew it. Kailey decided to pick the three of us up in her mom's car again. Fina helped me do my hair and loaned me one of her cool tops. I felt pretty good: nice boy friend, great sisters, and a very nice friend.

Kailey showed up around 9:00 p.m. She said hello to Mother, and then we all left together. Once we were in the car I asked Fina, though I already knew the answer, "Are you coming home with us tonight, or will you stay with Ian again?"

"Likely stay with Ian, but let me know before you go, in case I want to leave then."

"Okay."

As soon as we got there, Fina took off to sit with her friends from the lounge, and Ian. Aella, Kailey and I stayed together talking to Janie and a bunch of other friends. Kailey was right. Janie was over the fact that Cody and I were an item, that didn't take long. Despite the jealousy, I really did like Janie. Most of the staff were there, even the security guards dropped by to said "Hi," though they were still working, so they couldn't drink anything. It looked as though Janie had moved on from Cody, 'cause she was now hitting on one of the guards. She seemed to be having some success with the taller one.

It was about 1:30 AM when I heard a very familiar voice over the guard's radio. "I have a Code Brown in the lounge; could I get some back up?"

"We are on our way Cody," the taller one responded into the radio. "That's every night this week, the poor kid." The older guard chuckled as he spoke to the taller one who was with Janie.

He looked at Janie and said, "I'll be back this. Shouldn't take to long." The security guards started jogging back towards the clubhouse.
Janie walked over to us, "What is a code brown?" she asked Kailey and I.

Kailey spoke up, "It's usually an out of hand drunk. Poor Cody, he can sure get some Lou Lou's up there."

"Oh yeah, now that you say that Kailey, he had mentioned something about having a couple drunk guests earlier in the week," I said remembering our conversation on the beach.

About 10 minutes passed when I saw Cody come round the corner of the boathouse. We saw each other right away, and he set a course straight towards me. His eyes were fixed on me and mine on him. My attention was so fixed on him that, so unexpectedly, from out of nowhere, this woman stepped in front of Cody. She wrapped her arms around his neck and began kissing his cheek. Cody looked horrified! His eyes were still fixed on me. My expression was one of confusion, then fury like none that I had ever felt in my human form.

I'm not sure which was worse for him, the fact that she was doing this, or the fact that it was in front of me. She continued to paw Cody as though she were a cat, and he were her ball of yarn.

I felt my blood start to boil as she turned her face in my direction to see what Cody's eyes were fixed on. I realized she was the woman that Fina had described to us on Monday, the guest with half the ocean in her chest. She followed his eyes to mine. Her eyes were bloodshot and watery looking.

She was dressed as though her *hardware* were for sale. With her bright red lips she said, "Oh Cody, is this your little girlfriend over here?" As she spoke, Cody seemed to snap out of his trance that her arms had appeared to put him in.

My anger was boiling over. I stared straight at her she and could see I was livid, and she started to laugh. Cody tried to pry her arms from him, but you could see he was trying not to hurt her in the process.

The two guards came running from around the corner of the boathouse with her two friends trailing behind them. The guards had just gotten over to them when the strangest thing happened. This woman's chest started moving in a very…odd sort of way. She looked down. Her breasts seemed to move, as if they had a mind of their own as if someone else were controlling them. Suddenly they burst, like two balloons pricked with a pin. Her chest deflated to one that was smaller than mine. She screamed in horror. I don't think it was pain, just shock that her very expensive hardware upgrade was gone.

She launched into a full sprint back to the clubhouse with the guards running after her and her two friends following. As they ran, you could hear the girls calling to their friend, "Brooke, Brooke, wait for us." But I don't think Brooke felt like waiting at all.

With all the excitement no one was paying any attention to the ocean. It too was reacting to my instant fit of rage. The waves were huge, and now everyone was running for the clubhouse. Fina and Aella looked at me but I was already working on it. Trying to calm my breathing and heartbeat down, Cody reached for my hand and pulled me behind the boathouse with many of the other staff from the party. We heard the waves hit the front of the boathouse, shaking the little house where it stood. I moved in close to Cody with a look of fear consuming my face. With all the noise around us, of people yelling, waves crashing, Cody's voice in my ear sounded like a whisper, though I know he too was yelling. "What is it?"

"Someone's out there, I have to go help them. This is all my fault; I will never forgive myself if someone gets hurt tonight. Grab my clothes for me, please," I ducked around the corner of the boathouse, not giving him a chance to answer me.

Once I hit the water I knew exactly who it was, and where she was. I was beside her in a second. There was an odd sense to my ocean tonight, but I couldn't stop to focus on figuring out what it was right now. Janie was bobbing, then sinking, then bobbing again, trying hard to catch her breath. The waves were hitting her hard. I focused half my attention on calming the water and the other half on increasing her bouncy.

While I was doing that I was aware of Mother on the shoreline, out of sight of anyone from the clubhouse or boathouse. An eagle sat on her arm, and then the eagle took flight with something hanging from its mouth.

Once the eagle was over Janie it dropped; it was a life preserver. Though Janie had no idea, I helped her hang on to it, until the ocean came to a much more peaceful state. As Janie kicked her legs, I helped move her in to shore.

Cody, Ian, Fina, and Aella helped her up on shore. Aella took my clothes from Cody, and walked over to the bushes near the shoreline. Once behind the bushes she blew my wet clothes dry with a warm yet strong wind from her lungs and source.

I looked around before I darted from the water to the bushes where my sister was. No one was looking in my direction. Mother and the eagle seemed to be gone, and anyone that was left on the shore was standing or crouching over Janie now. I ran over to Aella and pulled on my clothes.

"Thanks," I said, "that was too close."

"You got that right. Did you see Mother and the Chief?" Aella asked.

"That was the Chief? The Chief of the Mi'kmaq tribe?" I said pressing the questions with my tone.

"Yes, I've gotten to know him quite well lately. He soars in my winds often," she smiled.

"I didn't know. Come on. We should join the others before they wonder where we are. I'm sure we'll have a family meeting tonight, no matter what time we get home. I'll worry about Mother then." I started out from behind the bush with Aella behind me. She scurried to catch up and walk beside me. Just before we reached the others, Aella said in a low voice, "Remind me not to make you jealous."

"No doubt," I agreed quickly.

Janie was lying on the ground, still breathing hard, but the colour had come back into her cheeks. As soon as I joined the group Cody came over and took my hand. Ian and Fina were now helping Janie to her feet. "Let's get you inside," I heard Ian say. Aella followed the three of them and I could see Kailey waiting for them over by the boathouse.

As I went to follow, Cody pulled me back. "We'll catch up in a minute," he called after them. Ian threw his hand up to let Cody know he had heard him.

"What was that?" Cody said, once they were out of earshot.

"That was a good example of my emotions when I don't keep them in check," I replied in a very short tone. "How could I let that happen, just that…that girl was holding you, she was in my spot, she had no right. I was so angry, so jealous! I've never felt that before." I finished feeling rather ashamed of my actions.

"That was all you? You caused all that over me?" he said, sounding like he disbelieved me.

"Yes, are you scared of me now?" I said sadly.

"No, just remind me not to get you jealous again," he lifted his eyebrow at me. "I thought Jeff and Craig the security guards had her. They were supposed to be taking her back to her room. She must have slipped away from them. Anyway, she's been bugging me all week. I'm sorry you saw that."

"You're sorry. I just about killed a co-worker and friend. I think I get to be the sorry one here," I said.

"Okay, I'll give you this one," he smiled a little and squeezed my hand. His look was soft and warm now. As he leaned over, I could feel his breath in my ear, "Why would I want a little Brooke when I have the entire ocean already?" he let out a laugh and finished, "Let's get you, your sister, and my sisters home."

"Oh, I almost forgot. Tonight won't be a good night for you to stay. Mother will need to talk to me about what happened and it's not a good idea for you to hang around for that. I'm sure tomorrow will be better if you want to come by in the morning, or afternoon, if you're tired." I finished, in a miserable tone at the thought of not getting the rest of the night on the beach with him, like we had done all week.

"Okay, so your Mother; she's in on all this?" he questioned.

"Yeah, but if it's okay with you, I'll explain all that another day."

"Deal," Cody smiled. "Come on, let's catch up with the others."

CHAPTER 11

Resisting Desires

Cody had us back to the cottage by 3 A.M., and just as I expected, Mother was waiting on the beach for us. She was sitting beside a man with a very weathered looking face, but he wore a pleasant expression on it.

"Is Janie alright?" Mother began, not addressing anyone in particular.
"Yes Mother, she is going to be fine. Thank you for your help tonight." I glanced at both of them, knowing it was me they wanted. My sisters hadn't done anything wrong, so I might as well be the one to speak. "Thank you both." Though I had never met the man, I could only conclude that this was the Chief of the Mi'kmaq tribe that Mother met with on occasion.

"You're welcome. That got a little…out of hand," Mother said, raising her eyebrows.

"Yes, I'm sorry," I bent my head, quite ashamed and embarrassed.
"Girls. This is Chief Grey Feather. He is one of the second plane Chiefs. He has been helping me watch over all of you. He has asked to speak with you tonight."

"Hello, Chief." We all said in unison. However, I wasn't done with what had happened earlier so I continued.

"Mother, are you sure we should continue with this plan? It would break my heart to have to leave Cody now, but I would do it if I was going to hurt others."

"Do you honestly think you could back out now, Naida?" her face was saddened. "Your ocean needs this as much as you and mankind do. Cody is your link, and your bond is strong. No, Naida, this is the way it is to be. Chief Grey Feather and I will do all we can to protect those around you until you can control your emotions, but you must not lose heart. I think you will find some new inspiration in your waters tonight, Naida." Mother finished speaking with a very heavy heart.

"Chief Grey Feather would like to tell you why he needs to help you. Please.
Could the three of you sit down with us." She motioned to the log, for us to sit on, across from them.

"I am honored to meet you women tonight," Chief Grey Feather began as he nodded at us. "As your Mother has already told you, I am helping her with your journey. Naida, however, I am helping because it is my duty in *this* life. My people have always tried to walk with you and not harm you. We respect your needs and know that you will respect ours. Each Chief, when passing on to the next level of existence, is given a responsibility until a new Chief can take over, allowing that Chief to continue on again to a new task, at a new level of existence. I remain to walk this earth and protect it from harm. As you know, our ocean is being harmed, and it is my belief that our Cody and his family are a very strong link to helping the ocean. You must not lose hope Naida, for Cody will find strength in it, and together all will be put right again." The Chief breathed deeply, "One other thing Naida, you must continue building your bond with the boy. I sense that a *test* is not far off, near the time when the seasons change, you will be faced with it. Be strong, Naida, I will not be far." And with his last word he bowed his head to us and within a blink of an eye, he was that beautiful eagle that I had seen on Mother's arm again. He took flight effortlessly, and disappeared into the night.

"Are you girls okay?" Mother asked quietly, as she began to build a fire in the centre of where we sat.

"Yes," we all said, one after the other.

"Good. Now go to your sources and be strong," she ordered as she lit the match of Fina's fire. Fina gave a little twitch with the striking of the match.

As we watched the fire grow, we all sat in a thoughtful silence. Moments later, when the fire had grown large enough, Fina disappeared into the blaze.

"Aella, stay close to Naida tonight. Naida, your oceans are hurting tonight, please…be safe, and stay with your sister." Her face was so worried looking that it frightened me.

Aella and I went to the side of the shore. Before I was ready, Aella was waiting in the wind. As I dove in, I immediately felt anguish surge through me. This must have been the odd feeling that I had felt earlier in the water with Janie, but now it had intensified.

I moved feverishly through the water searching for what was causing the feeling. I knew that when I came to it, I would know. I heard Aella, "Are you okay, Naida?"

"No, something has happened and I can't find the cause." I came to a school of fish. They told me some Trawler boats had been through earlier; they told me to go deep. My heart sank, because I knew what I would find. I had seen it before and it always left me hurt. Bottom Ocean Trawlers were the worst, but I had to go and see for myself, confirm what I now believed to have happened.

I went deeper, darker things became colder until finally I came to the floor of the ocean. The closer I got the more sadness filled me, until finally…there it was, or maybe I should say …wasn't. Nothing was left. The nets had been dragged along my ocean's floor taking everything with it. My beautiful cold-water-corals gone; they had been there for centuries! Young and old bottom feeders gone, and nothing left now to reproduce! My ocean being stolen from me before my eyes.

My anger started to boil again as it had at the party, but this was deeper, even more passionate to me. I let out a scream through my thoughts that surely the entire ocean heard. We would share each other's pain tonight.

I started to swim away from the ocean's floor harder and harder; I needed to get away. I reached the top and sprayed out of the water looking like water out of a whale's blowhole. Landing back in the water, I swam in circles; anger surrounded me and filled me. How could they take everything, most of which they wouldn't even use? The waves were massive now, but I didn't care. Then Mother's voice came "Aella, bring your sister back to me now. Naida do not argue, return now!"

"Mother, they have taken everything! Have you seen this?"
"Yes, Naida the whales showed me earlier through their thoughts. Come back." She pressed again, "Day will break and you need to get back. Cody will be here soon."

"Nice try!" I closed my thoughts and swam, swam with my fury as hard and fast as I could. I must have swam for 3 more hours before I decided to go in to shore. I was still fuming.

The sun was up now, and Mother stood by the shoreline with a bathrobe to throw around my body.

"Good. Now the humans can hear my yells, too. How can they do that? Those corals; and nothing left to reproduce..." my yells turned into sobs. Tears were now flowing down my face, "Why can't they see? Why? Why don't they care?"

I felt the gentle caress of a familiar hand on my hair pulling my head into a warm, comforting chest. I looked up, but it was difficult to see through the tears in my eyes, "Cody?"

He pulled my head into his chest again, "Shsh, we are going to do this together, Naida. You're not alone, and we will win." He was now lifting my chin with two of his fingers so his eyes could meet mine.

I saw the sincerity in his eyes and knew he would help. "Cody, it was awful, I can never get used to the sight of it." I felt weak, I didn't feel like I had been with my source at all. My knees began to buckle, but before I could slip, Cody had picked me up the same way I had him hold me in the water a week ago, except this time, I was not going to slide away from him.

He carried me over to the place where Fina's fire had been burning the night before, and sat me down on the log across from where Mother and Chief Grey Feather had sat. "Are you okay?" he breathed into my ear as he put me down.

"Yes...but no."

"Surprisingly I think I understand. Anna and I have been waiting for you for a couple hours now, so she had sometime to prepare me. I love you so much, Naida." He met my eyes with an intense gaze. "I was starting to worry about you," he said softly as he bent down and kissed me. His lips were so warm and loving that the anger I had still inside seemed to melt out of me into the sand. Though the only home I knew was my ocean, the touch of Cody's hand, and the warmth of his words felt more comforting to me than my home. We sat for a while in silence while I tried to push the thoughts of the night to the back of my mind where it would stay with so many other similar memories. Finally Cody broke the silence.

"I had an idea of what we could do today, but with everything you've been though, perhaps it's not such a great idea," Cody said softly.

"No, I think I need something to cheer me up, what was it?" as I felt a bit of a second wind kick in.

"Why don't you get dressed and I will take you into Halifax to buy a bathing suit. We can start your swimming lessons today." He smiled "Oh, and as long as the bathing suit is being purchased for my benefit, I get to pick it out," he finished with a devilish smile and one eyebrow raised.

"Okay, let me get my things, one second." I walked over to the little cottage, still trying to shake off the night of anger. Mother and Aella were inside talking.

I burst out, "Aella, I'm sorry I took off on you out there, it's just ..." She cut in before I could finish, "It's okay Naida. I've seen you like that before and I know my own limits." She smiled.

"Mother I ..." but Mother cut in also.

"Naida, you have a very good looking young man waiting to take you shopping. Why are you in here talking to Aella and I?" she smiled, letting me know everything was okay between us.

I got dressed and grabbed some money from the cupboard. "See you later," I called back at them as I ducked out.

Cody was waiting patiently for me outside. When I reached him, he put his arm around my shoulder and we walked up the hill to the car. The wind blew gently around us carrying the familiar scent of my ocean.

Once we were in the car on the way to Halifax, Cody reminded me of something I had promised to tell him. "So you said you would fill me in on your Mother being a part of all this. Are Aella and Fina connected to the water too?" he gave me a smile, keeping me to my promise "It looks like we have a few minutes so …" His wonderful mood was rubbing off on me, so I decided to start with my sisters, and tell as much as I could.

As I filled him in on Aella and Fina, his eyes would widen with questions, and then soften as I would continue to explain. When I had finally answered the questions that I knew would be brewing in his head, I asked, "So, did I miss anything?"

"Probably a ton, but I can't be specific right now." He smiled, laughed, and he continued, "You didn't tell me about your Mother. Where does she fit in?"

I smiled and assessed his expression: "Are you serious?" I said while raising my eyebrows. His face was still blank, so I assumed he was.
"Mother Anna Terra to you, or Mother Terra to some, or Mother Earth to others. Which do you prefer?" I just smiled and waited for it to sink in. Poor Cody had a lot to absorb. Cody's face looked as though he was still taking in what I had said, as we pulled into the parking lot of the mall.

The main shopping mall was located just outside of Halifax in Dartmouth. Mother had brought us here when we first starting living in the cottage. It was a great place to sit and watch people. I found it to be so interesting to see how people moved and interacted with each other. To see how girls would flirt with the boys, and the boy's reactions. At times it reminded me of a dance. To watch some women hurrying through with their children in tow, and others like they had nowhere in particular to be. Everyone moved differently, but much could be learned from their body language, and I was there to be taught.

Cody parked the car and we went in. Though the mall was a good teacher of mannerisms, I didn't like it very much. I found it very hard to actually look for one particular thing. People must become numb to the advertising in a mall. So many lights, colours, words on signs, everything competing for your attention. I found it best, as I had before with Mother, to put my head down and just follow. I put my hands around Cody's arm and moved in close to his body. He wrapped his arm around me as if to protect me from something bad. Little did he know he was just protecting me from sensory overload. It was so comforting how he seemed to understand my body language so well. He came to a stop outside a store. While his one arm was still around my shoulder, he lifted my head for my eyes to meet his.

"Are you okay? You haven't said a word, and your body is so stiff," he said.

"No, it's okay Cody, let's go look. What kind do you like?" I said as I walked into the store. So many colours, styles, he was going to have to pick because I couldn't filter through all of this.

"Well..." he started, as he set to work though the racks. He came up with three different styles and colours. "Do you want to try these ones on?"

"Sure," as I took them in one hand he led me to the back of the store where the change rooms were.

The sales lady looked quite concerned that Cody was about to accompany me into the change room, though he had no intention of it, that I was aware of. "Excuss me, only one person per change room," she flashed an accusing look at Cody.

"Of course, I'll wait right here if this is okay?" Cody gave her a very innocent smile and she grunted her approval. However, as soon as she turned, his eyes flashed over to me and that devilish smile was back on his face. I put the three bathing suits on the hook and pulled the curtain across.

The first one was a white with blue trim two piece bathing suit. It was cute, but nothing overly special. I opened the curtain and Cody gave me an approving look. "It's nice, do you like it?" he asked.

"It's okay, I'll try the next one."

A moment later I was standing with a one piece suit on. It was grey, with wide halter top straps tying around my neck, and a very low neckline. The leg holes came up high on my waist exposing all of my hip on either side. I looked at Cody "No" I said.

"Agreed" he replied very quickly.

The next one was a beautiful two piece suit. A familiar bluey-green colour with sequence detailing on the top that seemed to shimmer in the light. The top had one single silver circle to attach the triangles in place over my breasts. The bottoms were the same colour and made to sit low on my hips. The only detail on the bottoms were the silver circles around the hips which were like a belt. As I pulled the curtain back, the smile that I was beginning to really enjoy was back on Cody's face now. With the lift of one eyebrow he said, "Radiant!" However, the expression on his face said more about the bathing suit than his words did.

The sales lady was still keeping a close eye on Cody, and as she glanced to see which one I had on, her face seemed to look approvingly at me. "Ah, you found our Aquamarine Escape set. I love that one, and it looks beautiful with your eyes, dear."

I looked at the two of them looking as me "Yes, I think I will take this one, thank you."

We were in the car driving to our little deserted beach before I knew it. It felt good to be out of the mall in the car, just the two of us again. I was pulling the tags off the suit when Cody reached over and put his hand on my knee. "I wasn't kidding. You really do look quite radiant in that suit. I don't know if it will keep me focused at all." He laughed as we pulled into the parking area for the beach.

We took turns behind the sign getting changed into our bathing suits. He waited for me to finish. When I came around from changing, he took my hand and pulled me into his body. It was so warm and inviting that I truly felt I could stay there forever. This was an excellent start to my swimming lessons, because if I was going to resist the pull, I would need to really want to stay here, with Cody.

"So how is this going to work?" he began looking totally eager to get started.

"Well, I guess I will need to really focus on you and our connection. I need to ignore the ocean's pull, resisting that desire, and focus on quite another" I finished with my eyebrows raised as I scanned my *other* desire.

"Sounds good to me," and in one quick scoop I was in his arms enjoying the warmth of his skin on mine.

"This should work," my voice cracked with the excitement of his touch.

As Cody walked slowly into the water I thought of something, and I said, "I might not get it on the first try, so would you mind putting my suit on the nail behind the sign so I can put it back on."

"Sure, I guess." He was trying to sound disappointed but I knew he was just kidding around.

I held on to him, aware of his skin, his smell, and the intensity of his eyes on mine. I tried to feel him with every cell of my body. As my foot touched the water, my ocean pulled too. The desire to go to my source was increasing, but I was still in his arms still holding on around his muscular neck. He took another couple steps, and my knees and butt were now touching the water being pulled as if every ocean creature were enticing me to join them. They came stronger and stronger like waves crashing against the shore, and as the waves receded, the pull grabbed me and dragged me away from Cody. For the first time in my existence I was not pleased to be with my source. Damn! I watched Cody smile as he picked up my bathing suit and put it on the nail.

He went and waited for me over where we had started.
"Sorry" I said as I rounded the sign, adjusting my wet bathing suit.
"That's okay. We knew it might take a few times. This time do you mind if I fight back, though?" Cody said, smiling at me.

"What do you mean?"

"Well, I just think if it is going to pull you in this time, I should give it something to pull against. I'll fight for you, and I'll win." With that he scooped me up again, ready for the challenge. He started to walk slowly into the water, but before I could touch the water, he flipped me around repositioning me against his body so that my legs were around his waist, my arms around his neck, and my chest against his. Our eyes met, and he placed his lips on mine. I was hardly aware he was still moving into the water; I was just enjoying the intensity of his kiss. When we pulled our lips apart I realized we were up to our necks in water. Deeper than I had ever been before, without transforming! We gazed into each others eyes. "You're good" I said. I wanted, no I needed him, I could feel that now from somewhere deep inside. I slowly became aware that the ocean was pulling but it didn't seem like I had to go to it. It was as if I knew it would still be there when I was ready. Such a new feeling; I had no idea I was truly capable of having such unique feelings.

Cody held me tightly, as though he was worried a wave would whisk me away from him again. "How do you feel; are you alright?" He asked in a very compassionate tone.

"Yes, I'm…wonderful, and still with you. We did it."

He walked us out of the water. I remained tight to his body, not because I was worried about the ocean's pull this time, but because I was enjoying *his* pull so much.

"Should we try it again?" Cody asked.

"Yes, I think we should."

We ended up doing it five more times, and by the fifth time, I had become quite comfortable with the two pulls, and choosing which one to be with. I was feeling very proud of our success as we lay down on the beach together. "Wow, that worked out better than I thought," I said as I looked over at Cody's face. It was very serious, he didn't look like he wanted to celebrate like I did.

"What is it Cody, are you okay?"

"Yeah, it's just…I don't like the feel of it when you slip away from me. It feels like my heart is some how attached to you, and when you dissolve, a piece of me goes too." He finished and my mouth fell open. I had no idea how it felt to him. I hadn't even asked.

"Cody, is that why you fought so hard the second time?"

"Yeah, I realized after last week when you were showing me your connection, and how I felt after you slipped out of my arms, I would never be able to leave you. If leaving you felt anything like that did, I knew I couldn't bear the emptiness of it."

"Oh Cody, I'm sorry. I should have never asked you to do this. I didn't know what it felt like for you."

A wonderful smile broke over his face. "It's okay *Gills*, I didn't tell you how I felt 'cause I wanted to help; actually I wanted to win. And we did."

"*Gills?*"

"Yes, *Gills,* my little aquatic girlfriend," he laughed. "I was thinking that maybe we could go out for dinner and a movie, or something, tonight."

"Don't you call that a date, or something like that?"

"Yes, would you like to?"

"Sure, should I get changed?" I inquired.

"Well, I think if I took you out in downtown Halifax in that bathing suit, you would definitely get some looks." He smiled as he eyed me up and down again, and raising his brow he added, "I do like that bathing suit."

I sat up slightly and leaned over top of him, "Do I need something other than the jeans and t-shirt I was wearing before?"

"Nope, that will do. We'll keep it casual tonight. Are there any movies you would like to see?"

"Well, seeing as how I have never seen a movie, or had reason to see one before night, you pick." He sat up so quickly he almost hit me in the nose with his forehead.

"You've never seen a movie?"

"No, is that bad."
"Wow, Gills I've got to educate you." He pulled me to my feet and we packed up our stuff to get ready to go. I got changed behind the sign and as I did so, I looked out onto the ocean. Though I felt triumphant that I

had succeeded today, part of me felt like I had changed, and I didn't know if I was comfortable with that.

"I'm all packed up; are you ready to go?" Cody called. As I came around the sign I realized he was already changed and holding all of our things.

"Sure," I called back as I stole another look at the ocean before we left.

The dinner was wonderful and I'm sure if I had a need for food, it would have been very impressive. As for the movie, most of the time I just sat staring at Cody. It was neat to watch his expressions change with the different scenes. I had difficulty getting into the movie, but judging by the audience's reactions, it must have been good.

We went back to Cody's house after the movie. His Mom and Dad were just heading off to bed, so I wished them a good night before they left Cody and I on the couch in the living room. Cody turned on the TV and we watched some late night talk show guy. We didn't have a TV at our cottage; no phone, no TV. I guessed that I was unlike most teenage girls, but we didn't need those things to stay connected to each other.

Cody was getting tired, and he fell asleep several times with his arm around me. I didn't mind though, I just enjoyed being with him, and this TV thing was interesting. I liked it better than the movie. Before I knew it, the Sunday edition of Canada AM was on. They were talking about the weather and about an airplane that had to make an emergency landing in the Atlantic Ocean the previous night. All of the passengers were in lifeboats but the rescue ships were having difficultly getting out to them because the water was so rough they couldn't get too close for fear of crushing the lifeboats.

"I could help," I said out loud, and woke Cody up.

"What time is it, Naida?" he said rubbing his eyes to wake up.

"I don't know Cody, but I can help those people. Can you take me home?" I said.

"What are you talking about, Gills?"

"The people on TV; I could help them." He watched for a minute or two while it showed from a helicopter, 20 lifeboats or more being smashed by the rough waters.

"I need to help Cody, now."

"Okay, let's go."
We jumped into his Mom's car and drove to my beach. Once we got there I started to run towards the water, but Cody caught my arm. "Please be careful" he said as he assessed the crashing waves on the shoreline.

"I will." As I glanced at the waves I said, "You know those can't hurt me right."

"Yes, Gills just be safe okay."

"Okay," I replied and took off running towards the water again and dove in. I figured Cody could get my clothes for me again.

Once I hit the water I sensed an odd presence that was causing my ocean to stir, but before I could pay much attention to that, I needed to help those people. Within moments, I was underneath them trying to calm my angry ocean. It started to settle but there was still something else something wrong. I could now see the rescue ships moving in closer to the life rafts. They must have thought it safe enough to attempt a rescue. I could sense my angry waters weren't finished yet, so I tried to focus on calming them.

Most of the people were on board when I couldn't hold it anymore the last raft of people was flung high in the air, and all of the people were thrown out of the raft into the unforgiving ocean water.

I had to get those people to the rescue ship, but how, and what was causing this? I was able to calm the waters enough again to get the last of the people on the boat. It was essential that I find what had caused such a reaction in my waters.

I searched for hours but found nothing. I soared through the ocean for another couple hours hoping to come across something, and to store enough energy to last me while I was on shore. Still puzzled by the odd presence that had been so strong in my waters, I returned to my shoreline.

There, sitting on the rocks, was a fresh dry set of clothes neatly piled, waiting for my return. As I pulled them on, I could see Cody lying on the beach waiting for me. I could only guess, but I must have been in the water for four, maybe five hours. Poor Cody was still waiting! My footsteps were quiet on the beach so Cody hadn't heard me approach. He lay there so quiet and peaceful; I really didn't want to wake him so I decided to just sit down beside him.

Mother walked quickly and quietly over to where we were and sat down beside me. In a hushed voice Mother said, "Hi, he's been waiting for a while, he was worried about you," she smiled.

"I figured, but I needed my energy after I settled things down out there."

"Cody told me about the plane, and how you went in to settle the waters. I'm glad you did; is everyone alright?"

When she got the question past her lips, it was like a light bulb went on. "Yeah, the people appeared to be fine. They all got on board the rescue ships but…Mother are you aware of a new presence in my ocean. I mean, when I was out there today, it was like there was something else, or someone else."

TIDES

Her face hardened and her eyes narrowed. "What do you mean? What did it feel like Naida?" The change in her tone seemed to stir Cody a bit, but he seemed to stay asleep.

"It felt angry, vengeful even. I couldn't find its origin though, and I searched for quite a while."

"Hmm, thank you Naida I will need to speak with Chief Grey Feather but maybe until we figure out what it was that you felt…take caution when you join your waters."

"Mother don't be silly. My waters are the safest place for me."

"Naida…just be careful." And with her hardened tone, Cody did wake up this time. Mother stood up and gave me a look under her brow that I understood to mean she wasn't messing around.

"Hey, you're back…is everything okay?" Cody said as he sat up and rubbed the sleep out of his eyes.

"Ya, everyone made it aboard the rescue ship."

"That's great. I guess it wasn't easy. It took you awhile." Cody glanced at his watch.

"Ya, a little while, but I also needed to store some energy so I couldn't come back right away. Sorry," I said squinting my eyes a bit.

"Hey, don't be sorry…Anna and I had a nice chat until I fell asleep, I guess."

"She has that effect on people," I laugh. Cody slid over close to me and put his arm around my waist.

"So are you all charged up then?" he smiled and winked as he bent his head down and placed his lips on mine.

"Now I am," I sighed after he pulled away.

"So what would you like to do for the rest of the day? It's only…Two PM. Oh! I've been sleeping for a while. Hey, is it okay with you if we run my Mom's car back to her? I think she had some shopping to do this afternoon," he said looking totally surprised.

"Sure."

We got back to the house and met Cody's Mom at the door.

"Hello Naida, how are you?"

"Fine, thank you, Emily."

"Cody, you're really going to have to look into buying your own car," Emily said.

"Sorry Mom, I fell asleep on the beach at Naida's place. Here are your keys."

He gave his mom a kiss on the forehead and tried to look really sorry, but I doubted that she actually bought the look.

"I'm still waiting to hear back about that one on Carson's lot. Has he called back?" Cody said to his mom.

"No, not yet, but I'm sure that if he wants to sell it, he'll call soon," Emily said.

"Yeah, maybe I should call him again. I will tomorrow, before work."

Cody took my hand and led me upstairs to his room. "What kind of music do you like?" Cody asked once we were inside.

"No idea. I guess I like the stuff they were playing at the bonfire," I answered.

I walked over to his window and looked out at the tiny, well built tree house in the yard. His childhood must have been fun; his parents seemed so nice and his sister seemed to adore him so. What a great family. As I gazed though the window, my hand brushed something smooth sitting on the windowsill. When I looked down to see what it was, a flood of memories seemed to wash over me. I seemed to be staring through the object, not seeing it anymore, but watching all the memories this object had triggered.

Just then I heard some music coming from the other side of the room. I turned to find Cody sitting on the floor with a small white stick plugged into a larger system from where the music was coming.

"Hey what's that?" I said breaking out of my trance that the object on the windowsill seemed to have put me in.

"My iPod, I've got all my music on it."

"Really? It all fits in there? Hey I like this one." It was sort of a slow twinkling song that talked about *Home* a lot.

As he got up off the floor he asked, "Do you dance?"

"I don't know," I replied, not quite sure what he meant. I guess Mother hadn't gotten to dancing in our teachings before she tried to *integrate* us.

"Come here, it doesn't hurt...much," he said, smiling as he took my hands and placed them behind his neck. Then he slipped his hands around my waist, pulling me into him. We began to sway to the sound of the music. The side of his head was resting on the side of mine. I could feel his warm breath down the side of my neck. This dancing stuff was alright; much better than the movie thing.

"Do you like it?" Cody asked.

"What's not to like?" I smiled.

"I can't figure out why I felt so comfortable with you. Like I have known you for ever," Cody said.

"Because you have Cody," I paused for a moment before continuing. His door was shut so I knew we could speak freely. "Every time you looked out into the ocean you saw me. Every time you took a swim in the ocean I was with you. Your love for the ocean is a love for…me. The ocean and I are one and the same, so the comfort you find in the ocean, which I know you do, 'cause I can see it there in your eyes, you find also in me."

A few moments went by in silence when he said, "Why are the four of you here? Don't misunderstand me, I'm thrilled *you're* here, but why now, and why in Lunenburg, Nova Scotia?"

"Boy you sure can pick the questions, can't you?" I stared into his eyes now intensely, making sure he was okay. But he just looked curious, not weird or freaked just curious.

"We choose this shore in Lunenburg because …" I paused again for a moment, "well for two reasons really. The first being you. You see me clearer than any other human can, and that is because of our bond. Do you remember the first time we met?"

"Sure, but we didn't really get to meet 'cause you were on the floor before I could get a proper introduction."

"Nope. The first time we met was when you were three years old, Cody. Your Dad had brought you to the ocean to look for shells. You had your mind set on a blue one. That was all you said, *'Blue One Dad, Blue One,'* but you couldn't find one. You kept toddling up and down the shoreline picking up different shells and tossing them aside. I knew it would only take a minute to go and get one. So there I was in the depths of the ocean finding you a blue one. I knew the original occupant of the shell was long since finished with it, so I carried it back to you. With one wave into the shoreline I pushed it up in front of your little bare feet. You squeeled with such happiness, yelling for your Dad to come see." We had now stopped swaying to the music. Cody's face was straight, and I couldn't tell if he was focusing on the memory, or just getting weirded out. So I went over to the windowsill and picked up the beautiful blue shell that seemed to mean a lot to him. The way he had kept it all these years told me how much he valued it. I gave it to him for the second time in our lives. I decided to keep going with this memory. "After you picked up the shell, do you remember what you did?" I asked. Cody stood motionless, except for the one finger that he ran over the top of the shell.

"I crouched down to the ocean...to you Naida, and thanked you," he said very slowly, as if reliving the moment in his head.

"Yes, and you told your Dad that the ocean lady gave it to you. Do you remember that?" I inquired.

"Yeah, I remember telling everyone about the ocean lady."

"For several years after that, I would watch for you to come and play in my ocean. And every time, you would always say, 'Hi Ocean Lady' and we would play together, and when it was time for you to go, you would simply say, *'Bye. See you next time.'* I was convinced that you could see me, because every time you would stare directly at me when you said that."

"But what happened, why did I stop seeing you."

"I don't think you ever stopped seeing me Cody, you just stopped bringing me into focus as I became less real in your mind. The older you got the harder it was to believe your eyes, so you changed the focus," I finished.

Cody looked as though the wind had just been knocked out of him. He sat down on his bed. The music was still going as he traced his finger over the shell. I knelt beside him waiting for him to speak. I needed to let it all sink in.

About 5 minutes passed. He looked into my eyes, and as I looked back into his I could see I was coming into focus. He was truly seeing me for all I was and am.

He pulled me up onto the bed beside him and brushed his soft fingertips against my cheek. "I remember," he paused before continuing "but I thought you left me. I couldn't find you, or see you anymore." His face went totally straight and cold. "It was the same feeling I got when I couldn't hold onto you at the beach the other day. Like part of me was washing away."

"But I am here and I never did leave you. I didn't realize that you and that cute little boy on the beach were one and the same. I must admit, once you stopped seeing me, I thought that was it, and that would be the end of our contact or connection. I had put that memory away, all but forgotten like thousands of others, until your shell reminded me just now. During the last ten years of your life, my attention has been quite divided. I have spent most of that time trying to heal and help my waters. The deep sea trawlers and other things that humans take for granted in my ocean have done so much harm. I didn't expect the last decade to have made you so…attractive in every way. I'm glad the ocean has stayed so close to your heart."

"Wow! It seems every time we talk, we discover another bond between us," Cody said.

"Remind me, the next time I go into the ocean, I want to see if you can see me in the water; out of my physical form."

"Something tells me I will still prefer this form over the water form, *Gills*."

"Probably, but I would like to see anyway," I replied.

Cody laid back on the bed examining the shell, "So where did you go to get this?"

"Let me see," he handed the shell to me. "Oh yes, I went way out for that one. Remind me to show you on a map some day. It's a beautiful area."

"I wish I could see the ocean through your eyes Gills." Cody said.

"Hmm…that would be neat." I said.

"Hey Cody!" A voice came from the other side of the door with a knock. Not waiting for an answer, Kailey opened the door. "Oh hey Naida, I didn't know you were here. How are you?"

"Kailey; you don't just walk in, you know. You are supposed to wait for an answer," Cody's voice was a little sarcastic.
"Sorry," Kailey said.

"It's okay, and I'm fine. How are you?" I asked.

"Great. Are you staying for supper tonight?" Kailey asked.

"I hadn't asked her yet, but would you like to?" Cody added.

"Sure," I answered.

"Great, I'll let mom know when she gets back. I'm into a great book right now so I'll see you guys at dinner," Kailey said as she hurried out of Cody's room.

"Thanks Kailey," I called out to her. "Do you think she felt weird with me here?" I asked.

"Oh no, she loves the fact that you and I are together. She probably felt bad that she interrupted," Cody smiled.

"…but she didn't interrupt anything."

"Oh no?" Cody sat up and with the music still playing in the background. He got to his feet and pulled me up with him. Placing my arms back around his neck, he put his arms around my waist and pulled me in tight to his body. We began dancing to the music again. I felt so warm and content like this.

We decided to go out for a walk before dinner.

CHAPTER 12

Bonds

Cody and I returned to the cottage around 9:00 p.m. Mother was sitting quietly outside by the fire. She looked as though she was waiting for something. As Cody and I approached, I could see she was not alone. A beautiful eagle sat perched on her left arm. I looked at Mother, a little concerned with how Cody might react to the eagle if he knew who it was. As Mother stood to greet us, the eagle took flight. It lit over by the cluster of trees near the water.

"Wow Anna, that was a beautiful eagle on your arm. I hope we didn't make it go," Cody said, truly appreciating the Chief's grace.

"Oh no dear, it's okay…he's not really gone." She said smiling, but not really letting Cody in on the secret. "Please sit down and join us," Mother added. Then Chief Grey Feather appeared from the trees in his human form.

"Oh sorry, I didn't know you had company," Cody said.

"Chief Grey Feather, this is Cody Angel. Cody this is the Chief," I said quite sure Cody hadn't put together that the Chief was the eagle he has just been admiring.

"Oh, it's nice to meet you," Cody replied.

"And you also," said the Chief.

We all sat down, Cody slipped his arm around my waist as he pulled me in tight to his side. The warmth from his touch comforted me, and I hoped with every cell of my body that the comfort level would remain this way. Chief Grey Feather pulled out a long wooden pipe from his ancient-looking attire. He stuffed something into the end of the pipe, from his hand that seemed to be empty only moments earlier. As he lit the end of the pipe with a wooden match from a box that Mother had for our outdoor fires, all eyes seemed to be on him. A sweet woody smell filled the air around us. The smell was intoxicating. Mother and the Chief, however, seemed not to notice.

The Chief drew in a deep breath and broke the silence with his smooth, yet aged voice. "Naida, have you been in the water since we spoke?"

I knew he knew I had, but I went along with the conversation. "Yes, Chief." My reply came softly.

"And what did you find?" he continued.

Again, a question to which he knew the answer. "The deep sea trawlers were back." As I began I could feel my throat tighten and a lump begin to build. Cody's arm tightened around me, because he knew this was a sensitive topic for me to discuss so openly. He had no idea, though, how involved the Chief was already.

"And ...?" he pressed.

I looked at Cody. His eyes seemed fixed on the Chief for the moment.
"Something is building, an energy unfamiliar to me. One of anger, that I can't seem to pinpoint. Usually, when I am in my waters, if I sense

fear, pleasure or any other emotion, I can locate its source. Typically, I would find a boat capsized, with fretful people around it bobbing up and down. Their fear would act as a sound wave or frequency that I could follow to them. That's why it was so easy for me to find Janie in the water after the party. It's not like seeing with human eyes; it's a feeling that your entire being senses." I knew this explanation was more for the benefit of Cody than the Chief or Mother. I turned my attention to Cody. He was no longer looking at the Chief. His eyes were now fixed on me. I wished I could know exactly what was running through his head, though maybe it was better I didn't know.

"Yes, that energy is growing Naida, and it won't be too long before your test. You will need to pay close attention to your water because the source of the energy will reveal itself to you in due time." The Chief drew in a deep breath, only to let out a great cloud of smoke into the air after he finished speaking.

Cody sat quietly beside me, his eyes now looking a little foggy, and less focused and alert. I placed my hand on his knee. "Cody, are you okay?" I asked.

Cody's eyes were back on the Chief now as he slowly opened his mouth to speak. "How can I help, Chief…Anna?" as he moved his glaze between the two figures across from us, searching for an answer. "Naida can't do this alone, whatever it is…I will help." Cody finished.

The Chief sat up to his full, erect, seated height, appearing to scan the depth of commitment to Cody's last statement. Slowly the Chief began, "Yes Cody, you will help, and you're right, she can't do this alone. Your belief in your bond, the one you share with Naida, will prove to be the success or failure of this test. Though I have not created the test, I am sure the success lies within your heart." The Chief finished blowing out another great cloud of smoke in our direction.

"What do you mean Chief? I won't let harm come to Cody. Please, I don't want Cody to be involved in this *'test'* as you refer to it." My voice sounded like one of a small child pledging with a parent over something they wanted more than anything.

"Naida, the bond is not a short coming, and not one you should choose to protect like a child. Cody and you are stronger together than apart. It is your union that gives us hope of success." As he spoke, the great Chief got to his feet, his long ancient robe draped from his shoulders to his ankles. Mother also stood up beside the Chief, and for the first time since we had taken our seats around the fire, she spoke. "Naida, Cody, as I am sure you are aware of by now, your meeting was not one that was left to chance. No, I have known for many years that Naida's survival would be in question if left alone. And though there are many out there that possess a true love for the ocean, the Chiefs of past and present and I felt that Cody's heart was pure enough to endure this test, and the ones yet to come. Naida, this young man loves you for all that you are, and this is the bond that you so desperately seek. Do not try to sever it to protect him, as it will do all of us more harm than you could possibly imagine." As Mother stood shoulder to shoulder with the Chief, I became aware of a blue, almost magical haze around them. "The Chief and I have a bond not so different from the one you and Cody share. Together you can teach each other, and through your love for one another, you can grow and flourish. Without the love we share, we can't hope to survive." Cody and I sat beside each other, staring up at Mother and the Chief. As Mother smiled a warm relaxed smile at us, the Chief leaned over and placed a kiss on Mother's forehead.

"Good Night Anna, Good Night kids." The chief turned and stepped out of the light that the fire had cast around us. I was sure he was gone when I heard the gentle flutter of wings against the evening breeze.

"I'll leave you as well," Mother said and turned to leave. She turned back to add, "Naida, please go with caution into your waters tonight. Rely on your senses to guide you. Cody ..." Mother walked over to where we sat and she extended her arms to him. "Thank you, and know that I am always here to help you."

TIDES

Cody stood up and accepted Mothers embrace "Thank you Anna."

Cody and I sat quietly for a while, still absorbing the evening's conversations. Cody broke the silence, "Are you scared?"

"Only for you. I am what am and I have had some clashes in my existence. I don't understand what I am up against in this case, and it would shatter me if any harm came to you…Are *you* scared?" I said.

"Only of what life would be without you in my heart and in my ocean. Whatever is building out there Naida, I hope I'll be by your side when push comes to shove. But how will I know when you need me, and what can I possibly do to help you in the ocean? They have left so many questions unanswered. I don't want to fail you." Cody sounded more panicked now. I leaned over and put my arms around his neck, and he slid his around my waist.

"I'm sure you won't miss your cue. Don't worry." I leaned in and placed my lips on his, and he kissed me back.

CHAPTER 13

Struggles

"Are you tired?" I asked Cody, as he let out a big yawn.

"A little, how 'bout you?" Cody said.

"I could use a little dip. Hey, Cody once I'm in the water, will you come to the shoreline to see if you can see me?"

"Sure, but…what is it that I should look for?"

"Hmm, I think you'll know what I look like when you see me. This isn't the first time you've seen me in this form, remember?"

"Okay, but where should I look?" Cody asked, just to make sure.

"Come in a foot or so, and look around your legs." Before I could turn to head over to the cluster of trees by the water, Cody took hold of my arm and spun me onto his.

I loved this place, it was filled with such warmth. As my head rested against his chest I could hear the sound of his heartbeat in my ear. He

TIDES

wrapped his arm tightly around me, encasing my body within his. With the gentle kiss of his lips pressed against the top of my head, I felt the strength his love gave me. Like there was no test too big for us to handle. His whisper came soft and warm through my hair, "Hey Gills, please be careful tonight. I don't want to have to lie awake worrying about you. Though I may end up doing that, anyway."

As I broke away from his arms, his smile continued to warm me.

"Yeah, well you never know. I might find a nice whale to settle down with." I flashed him a smile in return. Cody bent over to slip off his shoes as he moved towards the water, and I towards the trees. Within moments I was dissolved into the water by his legs and feet. Now that he was connected with the water, he could hear me.

"Well, can you? Can you see me?" I thought for a moment he was going to fall over. His knees looked as though they couldn't support him much longer, and his eyes were fixed directly on me.

"Yes…you look…beautiful—amazing—like a hazy starry sky with a million glimmering lights. My G… I do remember this; that *was* you! Wow Gills, now I really won't be able to sleep tonight!"

"Well *get* some sleep; maybe you can just dream about me."

"Yeah, well, you be safe out there tonight, and I'll see you tomorrow," Cody said. I flicked two droplets of water onto his cheek. "Nice kiss Gills! See you tomorrow."

"Can't wait." I answered back. Then I turned and made for the open waters, but as I did so, I felt a heaviness in the waters around me. The Chief and Mother were right, its presence was growing, and whatever it was, it wasn't happy. I moved through the waters checking on many of the ocean creatures. They all appeared to be okay, as okay as one could be, when your home keeps getting violated. For the most part, everyone seemed to be moving more slowly, perhaps sadder as the time moved along. I searched all night for the source of the angry presence now inhabiting my ocean. I felt it so strongly now, but found nothing. It caused the waters to churn, and it was all I could do to keep them calm enough so that they didn't destroy shorelines. It seemed I was expending, almost as much energy as I was storing, from my source.

As the new day broke on the coast, I was working harder than ever to keep a calm within the waters. The sun was up, and I knew it was time to return to the cottage with my sisters, but I couldn't leave the ocean like this. Aella's voice came from above the water where I struggled.

"Hey, you're going to miss work…what's going on?" Aella said.
"Aella, you're going to have to tell Mother and Fina I can't leave the ocean today. Please."

"Naida, you know we can't spend the day with our …" but she stopped speaking, because another voice overrode hers in our thoughts.

"It was a tough night, last night," Mother's voice was strong.

"Yes, it's getting stronger Mother," I said.

"I can see that. You must stay with your source until it calms. Fina and Aella will tell them at work that you are sick. Come back in Aella; you can check on your sister when you return from work tonight," Mother said.

"Thank you Mother. Aella? Please tell Cody I'm alright; he'll be concerned when he finds out where I am," I said.

"Of course Naida, don't worry. Just take care of your waters and I will fill Cody in," Aella said.

The day seemed to go by slowly, I kept wondering if Cody knew yet. However every time I let myself get caught up in my thoughts of Cody, my attention to the ocean slipped, and I had to struggle to regain control of my waters. At times it felt like whatever this presence was, it was toying with me, as if it were forcing me to focus everything on the ocean. I swam with a whale family for awhile, until even their company became too distracting for me to maintain control.

Hours had passed and I was sure my sisters would be home soon. I moved in towards the land just close enough so that it would be easy for Aella to find me. A couple more hours passed and I wasn't alone any longer.

"Naida!" Aella said, her voice sounded urgent and worried. "Are you okay; has anything changed since this morning?"

"Finally, some company. No, everything is the same as when you left this morning. I still can't find the presence and it is still as strong."

"But you're okay, right?"

"Yeah, I'm okay. I'll tell you though, I never thought I would see the day when it would be a chore to stay in my ocean, but today…Aella? How is Cody? Did you see him? Is he okay?" I said, sounding a little panicked now.

"Yes, Yes, and Yes, though he is worried about you," Aella said.

"Well, I'll see him tomorrow and he can relax then. I wish I could see from the water, but it's too hard to see into the lounge from out here. Plus, I don't think the distraction would be helpful right now."

"Is it really that strong Naida?"

"Yeah, and I hope it to starts to settle soon." I said.

"I almost forgot; Cody asked me to ask you to met him on the shore of the beach club around 2:00 A.M. You can stay in the water; he just wanted to be able to hear you for himself. He's so cute, Naida," Aella said, laughing a little.

"Thanks Aella, what time is it now?"

"It's got to be around 6:00 P.M. Do you want me to ask Mother to let you know when it's close to two?"

"That would be great. Would you mind?"

"No problem. I'll be right back." Aella left in a gust.
Just then I noticed the water swelling around me and I had to turn all my attention back to the enlarged, pulsing, white caps.

Aella stayed with me for a good portion of the early evening. She kept me company as she had done for so many years. Though my focus stayed tuned to the waters, it was nice to have her nearby. I looked forward to Mother's reminder of the time, as I was sure Cody was keeping a close eye on his watch as well. Finally, Aella and I heard Mother's voice in our heads.

"Naida. It's 10 minutes to 2 o'clock. Cody is walking towards the ocean now..." but before she could finish, I could feel his presence in the water. He was connected to my source, and within a moment I was at his ankles, as he continued to wade into the water. I watched him as he searched the waters for me, and as his eyes fixed on me, I could see his warm smile break across his face.

"Hey, how was your night in the lounge?" I asked.

"Whatever...more to the point please; are you okay?" he said letting the smile on his face turn to one of concern.

"I'm fine. Like I told you before, there isn't anything out here to hurt me."

"Well, it sounds like the Chief and Anna would disagree with you, so stop trying to comfort me, and tell me the truth," Cody said.

But before I could reply Cody, was swept from his feet and pulled angrily into my water. I was so excited to see him that I had forgotten to keep tabs on my element. It was pulling him out fast and hard, and as my concern for Cody grew, it became difficult to focus on calming the waters. I focused all my energy but calmed it only slightly. I was going to need some help if I was going to save Cody and calm the water; time was of the essence right now. I let out a thought that I knew would bring my friends to my aid, and though they would likely frighten Cody, he would need to trust me. As I continued to focus on calming the water, a thought from a friend came to me. "Naida, I am here. What can I do?"

"Oh thank you for coming so quickly. Please, let him get on your back. Once he has some air on the surface, take him as close to shore as you safely can." I sent my thoughts to Cody's lifeline.

Now my thoughts were to Cody. "Please believe in our bond and let my friend help you, Cody. He will take you in as far as he can; please trust me."

Cody didn't respond, except for a nod of his head, and yet I knew he understood. He grabbed hold of the huge dorsal fin and allowed himself to be carried away.

I continued my fight to settle the waters and it was now starting to work. The swales were starting to calm down when my friend returned to me.

"He needed some help, but it looked like he made it the rest of the way to shore after I let him off. What is going on in here, Naida? Why is the water so angry lately?"

"I wish I knew my friend. It's not me causing it. By the way, how is your brother?"

"He's okay. The nets have left him with some very bad scars, but without your help that day Naida, he wouldn't be here at all. My family still thanks you."

"Well, now we are even, so Thank you my friend! Thank you. Please tell the other whales that I'm working on this anger, and I hope to find a source soon."

"Okay Naida, be safe—our love to you." And the great killer whale disappeared into the waters beyond me.

The waters were calm again, so I made my way to the shallows. However this time I didn't drop my attention from the ocean. As I looked up on shore, I saw Cody standing with Fina, Aella, Mother and the Chief. He was drenched and tired looking, but he was alive. I knew it was too dangerous to go in to close again. So I waited for Aella to join me and fill me in on the discussion from the shoreline. I was angry for letting Cody get in harm's way like that but I was relieved he was now safely on shore. It was now starting to torment me; how long would this struggle in my waters continue? It was standing between Cody and I. I desperately needed to resolve this so that we could be together again.

CHAPTER 14

The Calm

Weeks went by and the struggle continued. I refused seeing Cody when he made requests through Aella. I couldn't risk his life again like that. No, I needed to find out what was behind all this upset and anger. I searched harder than ever. With each passing day my mission to end this inspired me. I explored the waters of Florida, the waters of the Bahamas, from as far north as I could go, to as far south as I could go. East and west—nothing revealed itself to me. However I felt its anger in every corner. By day I would watch the trawler ships bring harm to my waters, and by night I would continue my hunt for the angry source that kept me bounded to my waters and apart from my new love.

Aella said that Mother had made up some story about me needing to leave Nova Scotia to go to a hospital in Toronto, Ontario. She had told my work that I was very sick, though it was nothing contagious, it was very serious, and I could only find the help I needed in Toronto. They seemed to buy into her story. Still I longed for the warmth of Cody's arms.

It was early September now, and though my struggle continued, there seemed to be a change in the waters. Aella joined me as she had every night since I had been bound to my task. Now that all the University students had returned to school, there were new faces at work, and this gave Aella and I other things to talk about.

Cody had also returned to school, along with everyone else. He still worked some shifts at the Beach Club, but he spent most of his days at school and his nights on my beach. Mother had set up a little study area for him outside the cottage. She even bought a small black and white TV at the thrift store. According to Aella, it only got three channels but it gave him some other distraction while he waited. Aella told me that Cody had bought a car with some of the money he had saved from the summer. Though I was quite thankful for Aella's stories of what was going on up on shore, I couldn't help but be a little jealous of my sister's freedom right now. I missed Cody so much.

"Hey, how are you?" Aella's voice came.

"I'm okay, how are you?" I ended my question there, though my sister knew what I really wanted to know.

"I'm fine. Thank you for being polite, but Cody is okay too. He asked me to say 'hi' and tell you he misses you. He has just settled into his homework up on the shore," Aella said. "Hey, do things seem really calm out here, or is it just me?"

"No, it's not just you; the waters have changed tonight. It scares me a bit because they haven't been this manageable in weeks. I'm not even sure I'm doing anything to control them right now." I said.

"That's great, isn't it?"

"Well, I guess so, but why would it just stop like that? I still haven't found the source of the anger."

"I don't know; do you want me to tell Mother?"

"No, not yet." I had another plan building in my head.

"Hey Aella, I think I will search the deep waters tonight. Go and enjoy your source for the evening. I'll be too deep to be much fun tonight." I kind of chuckled at the last bit, 'cause I hadn't been any fun since I had been bound to the waters.

"Are you sure, Naida? I enjoy being with you."

"Of course. Please go and enjoy your night, and I will try and do the same with this little break in the anger." I tried to keep my thoughts light so she wouldn't pick up on my excitement which was now starting to build.

"Okay, I love you, and be safe tonight," as she caught a gust, and took off.

"Love you too," I answered, not too sure if she heard me before she was gone.

I decided to hang around the area where Aella and I had said good bye, just in case she decided to check on me. After a little while, I thought it would be safe. The waters were still so calm, but I wasn't going to second guess it. This was the first break I had in weeks and I was going to take it. I made my way towards the shoreline with the little cottage on it beach. My excitement was almost too much to contain. As I approached I could see a figure sitting motionless in chair with a light shining into his lap, where I could only imagine a book lay. Beside his chair was a knapsack. Focusing hard on the water once more before I parted with it, I scanned the energy for any changes. It was the same as it had been earlier, so I popped out of the water by the trees. My robe hung waiting for me on a branch as it probably had, for most of my time away. I wrapped it around me and took a minute to scan the waters, but it was still just as calm with my absence.

Cody was still focused on the book, which lay open in his lap. He didn't seem to stir from it as I approached, likely assuming the movement, if he sensed it, was one of my sisters or something. In one fluid motion I had knelt down beside his chair. With my index figure pressed over his soft lips, I cupped my other hand under his chin. As his eyes met mine he let out a hushed gasp, and his eyes filled with the same excitement that my entire body was filled with. He jumped to his feet pulling me up with him, but before he could take hold of me, I grabbed his hand and pulled him towards the hill. Cody snatched up his knapsack and followed me up the hill quickly and quietly.

Once we were over the top of the hill and out of view of the little cottage, Cody couldn't hold it in anymore. He scooped me into his arms, and in a hushed voice he said, "I've missed you so much Gills. Thank god you're alright."

I was so overwhelmed by the warmth of his touch and the sweet smell of his skin that no words would come to my lips. However, I didn't have to worry about the loss of words for too long because within seconds his lips were pressed against mine in a kiss for which I had been longing. As we broke apart, a sigh of relief came through my lips. "That was too long to be apart." I said.

"Well, I've been right here waiting for you, Gills."

"I know, but this is the first break I have had to come to you."

"Did you find it? Is it gone?" Cody asked.

"I don't think it's gone and *no* I haven't found it, but for some reason it's decided to take a break tonight. So I took my chance while I had it."

"I'm not going to complain." Cody leaned in to give me another kiss, however this time, he stopped just short of my lips and looked around. "Wait. Come on. I have to show you something." Disappointed that he missed my lips I let him take my hand anyway, and hurry me over to a small car waiting by the curb. It was a baby blue bubble on wheels. Cody was beaming with a smile from ear to ear.

"It's a 1970 Volkswagen Bug. It needed some fixing, but it's almost done." He pulled open the door and gestured for me to get in.

"I like it; it's wonderful, Cody."

His face dropped a bit, "You like it? Gills don't you love it? I think it's great!"

I smiled and placed my hand beside his cheek, "Hum...I love you, I love Mother, I love my sisters, I love the birds and the animals...I love my ocean. I love everything that has life and the ability to love me back." My smile remained strong "I *like* your car." A look of understanding flashed across his face.

"And I love you, Gills." And before I could get in, he finished the kiss he was about to start before he thought to take me to see the car...

Cody started the car but before we drove away he looked at me. "How long can you stay?"

"I don't know, but just to be safe, let's not go too far."

"Is my house okay?"

"I think so."

He put the car into gear and put his hand on my knee. We were at his place in no time. "Can I get you some clothes from inside, or, wait a minute," he reached his hand into the back seat and pulled out an old sweat top and pants. "They're not to fashionable but they will be warmer than your robe."

"Thanks" Cody waited outside the car while I slipped them on. They smelled like him; something I had forgotten how much I enjoyed. We decided to head up to the tree house where we could talk freely, without the chance of his family overhearing us.

I sat up in the tree house with his head in my lap. I ran my fingers through his hair, just enjoying the feel of his hair and skin. We talked about everything from his school, to the presence in the water. The hours flew by, and then the sun began to shine through the doorway to the tree house. Cody's long legs dangled out this opening. I knew Cody would need to get ready for school soon, and I would need to check on my water.

Suddenly and involuntarily I let out the most disgusting cough that I had ever experienced. A black thick horribly-tasting liquid, erupted from my throat and mouth and landed on the floor of the tree house beside Cody.

"What was that?" Cody sat up startled by the sound, and banged his head on the roof of the little house as he did so. I just stared at the black stains on the floor, not grasping what it could possibly be. Cody had now slid out of the tree house and turned on the ladder to face me. His face was filled with horror.

"Gills, do you feel alright?"

"No," my voice was soft and wispy.

"We better get you back to the ocean."
Cody helped me climb down from the tree house. For some reason my knees were weak and my head was foggy. What was wrong with me? And all at once everything clicked into place. The taste, the liquid…my weakness. It was oil! Oil had been spilled in my water this morning.

"Cody we need to get back, *right now*."

"Okay Gills, we're going."

But as we rounded the corner of the Angel home, I noticed we weren't the only ones in a hurry this morning. Cody's dad was rushing out to his car also. With a muffin in one hand, a briefcase in the other, and his keys hanging out of his teeth, he was quite the sight. Cody was supporting most of my weight on his shoulders, while he tried to make his way to his car. Paul caught sight of us just as he got to his car. He dropped his briefcase, sending papers flying everywhere. However, Paul didn't stop to get them. Instead, he was by my side in a flash helping Cody get me to his car.

"What's going on Cody? Naida looks aweful!" Paul inquired.

"I'm not sure Dad, but I know her Mother will know," Cody said quickly.

"Right. I didn't know she was home from Toronto. Looks like you better hurry, Cody."
After Paul helped me into the car I heard him talking to Cody.
"I didn't want to wake your sister but I'm glad I got to see you, at least. Tell her that I will see you guys in a few days…maybe a week. There has been an Oil spill this morning off the Coast of Labrodor and they have requested a team from the University Science department to oversee the clean up and containment. It was a huge tanker ship…no one seems to know what happened yet. I've got my cell phone. Call me if you need me. I love you, and hurry Naida home, okay." He gave his son a quick nod and Cody was running for the driver's side of the car.

"Drive carefully Cody!" his father called as Cody started the car.

"Thanks Dad. I will. You be careful yourself, okay?" but he didn't wait for a reply. It felt like we were down the driveway and half way up the road in seconds.

"Naida, was that oil on the floor of the tree house?"

I nodded my head slowly 'cause I thought I might throw up if I moved it too fast, and I didn't want to take a chance of opening my mouth again.

Cody drove as fast as his little car could go with all the turns and bends in the road. By the time we parked the car, I was sure I would need to vomit. I waited until I was out of the car, and to the hedge that led into our beach, before I let it go. The sight of it made me gag even worse, but as my knees gave way to the weakness growing in my body, an arm caught me around the waist before I could fall. It was then that I heard the voices of my sisters and Mother coming, from somewhere up the path.

"This way Cody, we must get her down to the water. She can cope with this better in the other form."

I pressed my lips tight now, so Cody would have less trouble moving me, though he didn't seem to care about the mess I was making. He scooped me up with one arm behind my shoulders and the other under my knees. Once he had a firm hold on me, he ran faster than I thought possible. However, I realized that once his feet had hit the sand, Mother was able to help him move faster, the same way she moved me along the sand after the first day I saw Cody this past summer.

We were at the water's edge within seconds. Cody hesitated briefly before he continued into the water. I don't even think Mother would have seen it, but I felt it, and knew exactly what he was going through in his mind. He hated the feeling of me dissolving away from him. I looked into his eyes, "I'm coming back, you know."

"No, I don't know for sure." He measured his steps slowly now, unsure of whether letting me touch the water was really the best thing to do.

"We are in this together and I *will* be back. I love you."

A tear fell from the corner of his beautiful brown eyes and as it fell from his cheek, it landed at the base of my throat. Just as it touched he allowed my feet to make contact with the ocean. As I dissolved I heard him say, "I love you too Gills. Be safe! I'll be waiting."

Once in the water I was overwhelmed by the turmoil of the living creatures within it were in. Mother's voice came quickly, "Naida, do you know where to go?"

"Of course Mother, I'm already half way there. Mother, is Cody alright?"

"You take care of yourself out there and he will be fine. He will stay with us and I will keep him posted, okay?"

"Thank you Mother, but if …"

Mother cut me off before I could finish, "Focus only on your task and we will see you soon."

"Yes Mother," I replied smoothly. The closer I came to the site, the harder it became to focus on one thing. So many creatures were either dying or distraught for others that were stuck in the spill. Within seconds I was able to survey the size of the spill and the number of creatures stuck within it. It was huge.

I could make out the sound of a helicopter coming from above. I looked up hoping to see help, but it appeared to be a TV crew of some sort.

Mother's voice came again, "Tell me what is going on, Naida?"

"It looks pretty big and the waves are huge which isn't going to help the humans much. I will try to settle it down a bit out here, but I sense that presence again, and it much stronger than before."

"Did you think that it was gone?" Mother asked.

"I had hoped."

"That may have been what it wanted you to think. When did you leave the waters?"

"Soon after Aella had left me."

"Hmm, be careful Naida. It's more than just the spill you need to be careful of."

"I see that now…so stupid."

"No just focus now."

"There is a family of whales keeping to the outer perimeter of the spill.

Their thoughts indicate that at least two are stuck within the spill. I need to go and make sure the rest stay out. I'll update you in a bit."

I approached the family of whales and explained to them how they would only make it worse if they went in after their family members. I added that the humans would arrive soon to help them, and though they would likely need to take the oil-covered whales somewhere to clean them up, that they would be safe and would be returned to the ocean as soon as the humans could do so. I gave them my word that I would do everything I could to get them looked after and to get them back with their family. They continued to communicate amongst themselves and decided they had no choice but to trust me. I again tried to settle the waters with little success. They were raging out of control and I feared for the rescue ships now.

After a very long couple of hours I managed to gain some control. However, this seemed to anger the presence in the water. For the first time since I felt it come into the water, I was aware it's source was nearby. But I still could not pinpoint it.

I focused hard on calming the water even more but as I gained the source of the anger got stronger and stronger until it finally revealed itself to me. It was a female entity. She looked much like myself; a thought within the water. However there was *nothing* remotely pleasant about her.

"So you found me. But only because I let you. You're not very good at this, are you?" she paused. "I am Messina." Her thoughts were like razorblades. The hate within her was so strong.

"Why are you doing this?"

"Unlike you, I am not born of love and joy from the creatures within these waters. No, I am born of the hatred. The hatred they develop every time the humans rape our ocean for their greed. Every time they take all that they can, leaving us with nothing. I've even fed off some of your anger. Though it was very sweet, and to my liking it didn't last me very long. Not as long as the old coral they take. Now that is some lasting anger. I thought it would be fun to make you stay in the waters, chasing me while your love sits waiting for you to return. To watch you weaken without your human toy. But you proved to be a little stronger than I thought, and that game got tiresome, so I thought this might fun. I knew if I settled the water for long enough, you would take the bait and join your love, leaving me to do what I wanted. You're so predictable. So I sank a tanker while you were gone, giving me more hate and anger to feed off of."

"But can't you see? If you keep this up, everything will cease to exist…including you," I said now understanding the bigger picture.

"That will take a while, and it would be fun doing it. You've been growing weaker and weaker as the ocean creatures witness their continual destruction." She was right. I was weaker than I once had been. How was I to get rid of her? I needed a plan, and communicating with Mother without Messina hearing everything, was impossible. I could only hope Mother had heard everything, and was able to come up with something for me. I did have one ace in the hole, but if it would be strong enough, I couldn't tell until put to the test.

"You're right, I am weaker, but I'm not ready to leave my ocean, not yet. You have seen my anger for what the humans do to us. I would like to see how your plan unfolds, but as we agree...I have become too weak," I said rather defeated.

"Hmm. I can give you strength enough to see it through to the end, though it will be through my eyes," Messina said in a very sly tone.
"At least I would see it to the end; we are talking about the same thing, right?" I questioned.

"Merging yes; you are so weak compared to the strength I have stored. It would be easy, and I would leave just enough of you to see it through to the end. Yes I could do that, but I want one thing in return."

"What is that?" I asked.

"I want to leave enough of you in the merge to possess your human body for an hour or so, just long enough for me to crush your human toy's heart."

Messina's words sent a horrible feeling throughout my being.
"Not Cody. You keep it to the waters! Don't involve him!" I pleaded.

"That is the deal, or I just let you whither away to nothing. Your choice," Messina said.

I paused, considering all my options. Finally I said, "Fine, but if you're going to use my human body, you're going to do it now."

"Deal." Messina's voice sounded triumphant.

Before I could think another thought, she was on top of my being, sinking slowly into me. The cold hatred seemed to consume every part of me. However, she was careful to leave just enough so that I would be able to form my human body on shore. With a speed that was faster than what I was used to traveling at, we arrived back at the beach within moments.

Before we got out of the water, I told Messina, "If you want to be convincing, as I'm sure you do, put the robe on. He won't pay attention to your words without it."

"You're probably right, and I want him to hear every word I say," she said as we climbed out of the water pulling the robe around our body. I was now like a visitor within my own skin; she possessed most of the room within the body. I could not control the movement of the limbs nor could I control the words that my mouth would speak. I could only see what she was seeing. I was preparing for the bit of my heart that was left, to be broken along with Cody's.

As we walked up the beach, a single figure stood by the cottage alone, waiting. I heard the voice call out, "Naida, thank god you're okay." Cody's voice was warm and inviting, though his steps were slow as he moved towards us, and us to him. I could feel Messina's heart rate quicken as we drew nearer to Cody. She let her temper and anger for the human race rise. Like a pot of boiling water bubbling and spitting, she was prepared to scald the man that was my true connection to the human race and my ocean's survival.

Inside Messina, I was screaming out of fear, but that only seemed to feed Messina's boil. Her steps grew faster as she prepared to drench Cody with her anger. I struggled to take control of our body but it was no use,

I was too small and weak to overtake her. I heard Messina once more, "Can you see him Naida?...HA, I know you can, and trust me, I won't give up until he looks at us with as much hatred as I have for him and all his race. Are you ready, sweet little Naida?"

I let out one last scream in her head and then she began, "You bastard! Have you seen what you and your kind do to my ocean? I hate you and everything about you and your kind." Her voice was harsh and unforgiving, but Cody didn't break his stride. He kept walking straight for us.

"I'm sorry you feel that way, but I do love you," he said. There was only a couple feet between us now, and I longed for his touch though I knew Messina would hate it, and not allow it. No, she was looking to shatter him.

"You're such an idiot. You think you can just exist, never giving a crap about what you do to the world around you. Well, guess what? No human is welcome in my ocean from this day forward. I will take pleasure in crushing anyone who tries to enter it."

Cody's voice came softly, "Naida, I care what happens in your waters and you know that I am working hard to find ways to help them. You know I love you." As Cody spoke I felt as though there was more room in my body for me. Which meant Messina was getting smaller. She obviously connected this at the same moment as I did, though her arrogant nature caused her to try again.

"You have done nothing but harm. I could only ever feel hatred for you. You take things that aren't yours to take. You harm all of the creatures in the ocean, and they all hate you for it. If you step foot in my ocean, I will take pleasure in killing you." Messina scanned his face for a change but saw the same warm, inviting eyes that she had seen before she began.

TIDES

Now it was Cody's turn, "I love you Naida. I love all that you are and I will continue to make your waters safer for all who live within them." As Cody made his move, so did Messina and I along with her. Cody moved in to slip his arms around our waist, but Messina was slightly faster. She moved back out of his reach. With Cody's last 'I love you's', I was able to occupy more space than before, and Messina felt it too. She was done; she turned on our heels and made for the ocean. However, we couldn't see the ocean when we turned. Two figures stood shoulder to shoulder blocking Messina's escape route. Then I felt the touch I so longed for; two warm strong arms surrounding my body. Messina struggled to get free but Cody had made sure he had a good hold on us. I felt his love thaw the cold hatred that possessed my body. My space grew quickly and as Cody was melting it from the outside, I now occupied enough space so that I could also melt it from within. Cody spun me around to face him, and as he did so, our eyes met; this divulged to him that I was back. He placed his lips on mine, and as he did, I felt the last of Messina melt away. She had played right into my plan, and Cody and I had passed the test. A small ugly thought crept into my mind. *'If this was a test then what was it preparing us for?'* I pushed the thought to the back of my mind, because for now I was going to enjoy the moment.

CHAPTER 15

The Team

My body felt weak but I didn't want to let go of Cody, not yet. He kept his arms around me, likely aware that he was the only thing supporting me from falling flat into the sand. Mother and Chief Grey Feather were standing behind me. Cody turned slightly so that I could see them too.

"How do you feel Naida?" Mother was first to speak.

"Weak, but whole again…some presences?" I stammered.

Chief Grey Feather lit his pipe and blew the smoke around Cody and I. The chief's voice was soft, "Strong but not strong enough. She's gone." I didn't realize it at first but he was using the smoke to check the perimeter around us. He seemed satisfied enough, so he then stopped blowing the smoke around us.

"Thanks, I mean, Thanks everyone."

"I almost blew it," Mother began. "But it has always been my practice to give a little listen before piping up in your head, just in case you were in the middle of a conversation. In this case it was a good thing. I figured you would know I was listening when I was quiet for so long".

"Thank goodness she was, Naida. When you came out of that water every inch of me wanted to believe it was you, and if Mother hadn't prepared me as she did…well …" Cody eyes flashed to the sand under our feet. "I had to keep telling myself that it wasn't you saying those words. If I hadn't I'm sure I would have been too upset to have stopped you from getting back in the water. Her eyes were so cold and black; it made it easier to remind myself it was her, and not you."

Just as Cody finished speaking, a familiar voice called out from the cottage,
"Hey, if you guys are done chatting, could you come here a minute." Aella had stuck her head out the cottage door and was waving for us to come to her. Cody decided that I was still too weak, or that he just didn't want to let go of me yet, so he scooped me up as he had earlier that day and walked with the Chief and Mother over to Aella.

Once all of us were in the little cottage, I realized just how small it was with 6 adults all huddled inside like that. Fina and Aella were watching the small TV mother had bought for Cody while I was away. The images on it were horrifying. While we were dealing with Messina, I had almost forgotten about the oil spill. However, the little TV was keeping Aella and Fina up to date.

"What have we missed?" Mother asked my sisters.

"Well, it's so hard to tell, but we can only assume that the whales are still stuck in the spill. The reporter isn't saying much about the aquatic life in and around the spill. The whales are likely confused by now. I don't think they know which way is safe," Fina said.

"My dad is on that ship. I'm sure that is the one they dispatched his team to." Cody said. I needed to help them, and this could be a good link. As I looked at Chief Grey Feather, I could tell his mind was going in the same direction as mine. He raised his eyebrow and gave me a reassuring nod.

"Cody, I need to get to the water. Can you …" but before I could finish, Cody had cut in.

"You are too weak to go back out there right now. No, it's too much," Cody said narrowing his eyes at me.

"Cody, where do I get my strength from?" I questioned him.
My voice became a little more forceful this time, "Messina is gone and it looks like your father could use some help. So are you going to help me to the water, or do I have to crawl there myself?"

He looked into my eyes and decided not to argue any longer. Without a word, we were out of the cottage on our way to the water.

"Do you still have your phone with you?" I asked.

"Yes," he replied. We were just feet away from the shoreline now.

"Good. Keep watch on the TV, and if I have any trouble getting the whales to cooperate, we may need to talk to your dad on the ship. Mother will keep you up-dated."

"Be careful Naida. I love you." He winked his eye and gave me a kiss. His lips met mine and for the second time that day, he let me touch the water and dissolve away from him.

"I love you too. I'll be back before you have time to dry your feet off," I said while he remained connected to my source.

I moved quickly and silently through the water to the oil spill. Even with the spill, and the fear from all the creatures affected from it, the sense of anger and rage that I felt earlier was gone. For the first time in quite a while I sensed a common united fight. The loving energy from the humans working on cleaning up the spill, and the creatures trying to guide and encourage each other, was giving me an overwhelming amount of strength.

Mother's voice broke into my thoughts, "How do you feel Naida?"

"Strong! I can see the humans working to control the leak from the sunken tanker ship, and they have contained the spill on the surface. They must have been pretty quick because the spill hasn't gotten too big. Their energy is so good and loving, I wish all humans cared this much."

"Cody wants me to tell you he wishes he were out there with you," Mother said.

"Are you still watching it on the TV?" I asked.

"Yes"

"Good. Stay tuned. I will talk to you in a minute."

"Okay, we'll be here," Mother said reinforcing her support.

I had just spotted the two whales that I had told I would come back and help. They were waiting underneath the location of the spill. One was looking very weak; the other was encouraging the weak one to hold on.

"You're back," the strong one addressed me with relief in his thoughts. "I told you she would be," he finished to his sister. "This is my sister, CoCo, and I am Deuce."

"Hi Deuce, CoCo, thanks for staying, but it made it easier to find you. It was a bit of a struggle, but yes, I'm back. So I need you to explain to me what happened, and how you ended up with the oil on you, and not the rest of your family," I said to the whales.

"Well, the waters were getting violent so we were headed to a spot where we can avoid ships like these. This tanker was off course from where they usually go by quite a distance. Anyway, we saw it start to go down, and as we went up to grab some air, its spill had already started. My sister broke through the water first, and I'm afraid she got the worst of it. Though she did save the rest of the family by telling us something was wrong before we could break the surface. I was right behind her and though I got it on me, I don't think it's in my blowhole yet. We have been up for air twice, but we tried to avoid the oil above. We thought we should stay close to where we saw you last. CoCo had almost given up hope, but I knew you would be back. So what do you need us to do?" Deuce finished, sounding ready for the next step.

"Well, first you need to trust me, and understand that the humans that are helping to clean up this mess are not the ones that caused the harm to our waters. Just as there are good and misguided presences in our waters, there are good and misguided humans. Some want to help our waters, while others care only for their financial wealth. I will explain that some other day. Just know that not all humans have the same intentions or motivations. Do you feel the love underneath the fear in the water now?" I asked.

"Yes," they both said in unison.

"Good. Do you trust me to guide you?"

"Yes," Deuce said on his own.

"Okay then. Mother are you there?" I asked.

"Yes Naida, do you have a plan?" Mother's voice came so the three of us could hear her.

"Is that Mother Terra?" Deuce asked.
"Yes. She is going to help us," I said. "Ask Cody to get his father on his cell phone, please."

"He is already on the phone with him Naida. He has been for about 5 minutes already. Apparently, his team is on a new ship. They have been trying to get your friends to come close enough so they can help them, but they are staying to deep and can't."

"Ask Cody to find out what they need the whales to do and where they need them to go?"

A few minutes passed and Mother's voice came again. "The ship he is on can only accommodate one whale at a time, but they have a spot to load the whales in and clean them up. They will then move them to a spot that's safe. They know there are two whales, so they will go as fast as they can so they can help both."

My attention turned back to the whales now. If I took CoCo to the ship first, it would take them longer to help her, and Deuce might become worse off. If I took Deuce first we might lose CoCo while they were cleaning him up. "Well, who is going first?" I asked, hoping the answer would be clear for them.

"CoCo. I can wait," Deuce said.

"No, I'm too scared, and what if their intentions are of the misguided nature. No, I don't think it's safe," CoCo said.

"I can assure you and I would not mislead you on this. Their intentions are those of good. What if I came with you? I can take my human form, if need be, and help them."

"I'm scared Naida; I've seen so much harm," her thoughts were low and timid.

"I understand, but I will not allow harm to come to you. Like I asked before, you need to trust me."

"Please go. You need their help," Deuce encouraged.

"You will come with me, Naida?"

"Yes, I promise to stay with you," I said, now directing my attention back to Mother. "Is Cody still on with his father?"

"Yes, but his father is becoming impatient with him, so let's get a move on," Mother said.
"Ask Cody to tell his father to move the ship in as close as he can to the oil spill. Find out where the whale is to enter from?" A moment or two passed as we waited for the reply.

"Sorry. Cody had to convince his father to trust him that the whales would be easy to help if he did as he said. Cody had to promise to explain all this later. There is a huge door on the bottom of the ship. It will open and lower a platform. Tell the whale to swim on to it once it is lowered."

"Okay," I answered as I turned back to the whales, "Are you ready?"

"Stay close to her Naida; keep your promise," Deuce said.

"Let's go," I said to CoCo, and turning to Deuce as we started out, I said, "I will be back for you soon."

"Thank you. I will be here."

We made our way to the surface and saw the ship waiting. I said,"Mother, tell Cody we see them." Just then the door opened and the platform lowered as they said it would.

"Don't leave me," the whale said with fear in her thoughts.

"I'm right here. Come on. I think the platform is down far enough."

We swam over to the platform and CoCo swam right onto it.

Mother's voice came again, "Alright. Cody's dad has no idea how the whale is doing exactly as it's supposed to, but we will deal with that later. Keep it up, Naida."

"Thanks. We are ready when they are," I said, and just then the platform started to move into the ship. Once we were up we could hear the doors lock, and seal the whale, water and myself inside. Just then a loud sound began, and the water level began to drop.

"Mother, ask Cody what's happening."

"Cody said they are going to let half the water out. You should see platforms in the room upon which the humans will be able to stand in order to be beside CoCo."

"Okay," I said.

I could sense CoCo's heart beating fast with fear as the water dropped around her. As soon as the water was at half, the noise stopped. Several lights went on around us, the door in the room opened, and several people entered.

"I'm right here beside you; don't be afraid," I said.

"Thank you," CoCo said.

I looked at all the people now looking at CoCo, none of whom were moving to help. Most of the faces seemed so young and in awe of being so close to such an amazing mammal.

The door swung open and one more person entered the room. It was Paul, Cody's dad. He was pulling on a long white lab coat.

He began to address them, "Alright. We need to assess the damage and get her cleaned up." As he continued to direct them, it occurred to me that I could help speed this up by telling them what they needed to know, but Paul couldn't see me. Not the way his son could, and he wasn't connected to the water, so he wouldn't be able to hear me either. If I transformed into my human body, I would be naked, and too much explaining would need to happen before they would be able to help CoCo.

"Mother, are you still listening?"

"Yes Naida, what is it?" Mother said.
"Ask Cody to call his dad again. He needs to know all that has happened to CoCo. It will be more efficient if I can communicate between Paul and CoCo."

"Okay, just one minute. He's dialing." I heard Paul's cell phone ring and he let out a sigh, apparently annoyed at the sound of it.

"Yes, Dr. Angel here?" Paul said. "Yes Cody? No, I think we've got it from here buddy but thank you for your help. I don't know how it worked, but we've got her here. She looks pretty rough but…what…how can you know? Cody, come on …"

"Mother, tell Cody to tell Dr. Angel to touch CoCo's nose and watch her left eye." I said.

"When he touches your nose, close your eye, and open it again," I said to CoCo. Paul let out another sigh and walked to the front of the beautiful whale, and placed his hand on her nose. CoCo slowly closed and opened her frightened left eye.

While they were convincing Paul that communication between he and CoCo was possible, I was busy filling Mother in on what had happened to her, and how she felt. Once Paul was convinced, Cody continued to fill him in on everything I had told Mother.

"Cody you're going to have a lot of explaining to do when I get home." Stated Paul. He seemed comfortable enough to trust what Cody had told him so he directed his team and they set to work on cleaning the whale up.

They worked hard, and at one point I heard one of Paul's team members say to him, "I wish she would open her mouth so we could see inside it. That would be such a help."

I told CoCo to open her mouth and not to close it until I told her to. As she opened her huge mouth, I thought the boy that had said that, was going to fall over.

"It's like she can understand us," the boy said as he started to check inside her mouth. The team continued cleaning her non-stop until they were sure they had everything.

"How do you feel?" I asked the whale.

"They have forgotten a part of my blowhole; I can feel the oil still on the rim of it," was her reply.

Once again I contacted Mother and filled her in, and the sound of Paul's cell phone came again.
"Cody, she has been calm enough that we haven't needed to tranquillizer her, and to be truthful I haven't wanted to. I don't think her vitals could withstand it. I can't ask someone to get up on her to do that." There was a pause in Paul's speech, and then, "Yes Cody, I do trust you but …"

"Okay…Okay I will do it then. I can't ask any of my team to do something so dangerous. Are you sure?"

He hung up the phone and moved towards CoCo, again placing his hand on her nose. She winked at him again and moved her head down as low as she could in the remaining water. He took up the supplies he would need and started to climb up on the head of the whale, making his way to her blowhole. She remained calm and let him finish cleaning her. As he was getting off, Paul had the most amazed look on his face. "I don't know what this is all about but I intend to find out," he said under his breath.

He touched her nose again, and she simply bowed her head in thanks. And without my translation this time, they seemed to understand one another.

Paul was the last to leave the room before the room began to fill up with ocean water again. Then we heard the sound of the doors being opened and us being lowered back into the open water. The water all around us was clean salt water, and as the platform clicked into position, the great whale moved off into the ocean.

"Mother, tell Cody to tell his dad to move the ship back to the same place as before, where they had picked us up. I will meet him there with her brother," I said.

"Okay Naida, be swift," Mother said.

"Come on Coco, we need to find your family so I can get back to Deuce. He will be so happy to hear you're fine," I said as I lend the great whale away from the ship.

I searched the waters and honed in on their location within seconds. They had stayed close knowing that I would keep my promise to them. Good thing all had gone my way with the situation on the beach earlier.

Within a couple minutes CoCo was back with her family, and I was free to turn to her brother.

It only took me a few seconds to get back to him. I was shocked when I saw him. He was barely alive. The sound of his heartbeat was slow and irregular. I entered his thoughts, "Deuce, can you hear me?"

"CoCo, is that you?" Deuce's thoughts were slow in my mind.

"No Deuce, it's me Naida. CoCo is back with your family. The humans cleaned her up and released her. I've come back to help you get to the ship; they'll take care of you there," I said, not entirely sure how I was going to get him there.

"She's alive then? She made it Naida?" he sounded a little happier but still more labored and distressed then he should.

"Yes Deuce, she is fine, and they can't wait for you to join them so you all can continue on your way. Can you make the journey to the ship now?" I asked.

"Oh Naida, I don't know, I..." Deuce began, but I cut him off before he could finish.

"Deuce, we must try...please. I made a promise to your family that I would do everything I could to get you back to them. I intend to hold up my end, and I think you still have some fight left." I tried to make my thoughts less pleading, and more light, though I'm sure he heard right through me.

"I took more in my blowhole than I thought I had Naida. It feels dreadful," Deuce said with a distasteful look in his eyes.

"Mother?" I said.

"Yes, Naida?" Mother's voice came quietly as though she were waiting for my signal.

"Ask Cody to call his Dad; explain what we are facing. We'll need the ship to be totally ready for us. Paul's team will need to move fast once I get Deuce there. Even then I'm not sure ..." my thoughts trailed off.

"Naida, do the best that you can. Cody will make the call now. Good Luck," Mother said.

"Thanks," I said to Mother, turning my attention back to Deuce.

"You ready?" I said.

"Naida, I will die trying, but I *will* try," Deuce replied.

"Okay, let's go then." Deuce was slow to start, but with what appeared to be great effort, he began shifting his beautiful black and white body into motion. We must have looked as though we weren't moving at all, but we did manage to gain some ground. I became aware of the presence of the ship, which seemed to be about ¼ of a kilometer away from our location.

"Mother?"
"Yes, Naida"

"Can you ask Cody if there is any way they can move it in closer? Deuce is having a hard time moving!" There was a short pause, before Mother replied.

"They're moving in. It will only take them a couple of minutes to be close enough to you. They can see Deuce on the sonar. Can you get him to start surfacing?" Mother asked.

"Okay," turning my attention back to Deuce, I answered. "We need to head to the surface now; are you ready?" I waited, but Deuce didn't respond to my thoughts.

"Deuce, come on I can see the ship. It's right there. Let's go. Please Deuce." My thoughts were now starting to sound a little more pleading than I wanted, but his now motionless body and lack of communication was starting to scare me.

"Naida, I can't. I can't do …" Deuce began, but before he could finish, he started to move towards the boat, which was now in a good position and within full sight. Deuce moved faster than I would have thought him able to. A voice entered my thoughts just then: "Come on. We don't have time to waste." I turned and looked. It was Deuce's Mother. She had been obviously keeping in contact with our communications and she came to help.

We were in close to the ship when Deuce's body seemed to go limp. His Mother seemed to be using all of her strength to move her son up and over the platform underneath the ship. Within seconds she had him to the platform, and he inched his way onto it with the little strength he had.

"Naida, you stay with him like you did for CoCo. I fear for him," Deuce's Mother's thoughts were quick and distressed.

"I will. But we could have made, it. You shouldn't have come. Now you have endangered yourself."

"I won't surface here. I will clear the spill before I break the water. Please, just look after my son."

"You are already too close to the surface; you must …" but his mother didn't let me finish.

"The platform is rising. You must hurry now. I'll contact you or Mother Terra if I become ill in anyway. Deuce is part of my heartbeat, and I can't bear the thought of losing him. Please, do all you can Naida. Hurry now; the platform is almost in the ship."

She was right. They would be shutting the doors soon, and I needed to get in there. I made it in just as the platform locked into place and the doors began to shut. I was barely able to detect Deuce's heartbeat. His thoughts were faint. "Naida, tell my Mother thank you, and that I love them all."

"Oh No Deuce; this is not over yet! The humans will help you. You can do it. Please Deuce, don't give up." As the load noise started and the water level began to drop, I knew Deuce was going. I felt his presence brush over me. For one last time his thoughts came to me. "Thank you Naida, may love live strong within your waters always."

Though the huge motionless body lay next to me, he was no longer in it. He was now part of another existence, and had left me on the ship.

As the door to the room swung open, I knew the humans too would soon know he was gone. However, in this mad rush, the humans were all running around doing things to Deuce's lifeless body. Paul was yelling at them to do this and that, none of which I understood. Did they not understand Deuce was gone? Each time they poked or touched him I felt myself get angrier at them for not understanding. I heard my thoughts yell out for all the ocean to hear, "STOP, JUST LEAVE HIM ALONE."

I became aware of the ship swaying quite violently now. The humans stumbled around trying to hang onto handrails, while other objects that weren't being thrown around on the ship. I heard Paul's cell phone ring despite all the yelling and commotion. Paul spoke on the phone for a moment, then closed the phone and began to yell over everyone.

"Everyone out! Go back to your posts on the ship. We can't help this whale now." Many of the students stopped and stared at Paul.

One woman who had been quite forcefully trying to push a tube into Deuce's mouth yelled back, "But Paul, we have a chance still to save him…just wait."

"No, everyone out," Paul said even more forcefully. With reluctance, even the pushy woman, left the room behind the others. Though, she made sure she was the last of the team to leave, aside from Paul, just in case he changed his mind. The room became calm, and as it did, I too became calm. The ocean settled along with me.

Paul removed his lab coat and placed it on a post near the water. He began to speak, "Ah, I am not really sure what's going on here," Paul began uncomfortably speaking aloud, to what otherwise, looked like an empty room other than the lifeless whales body in the centre of it. "But if what my son tells me is true, and so far he hasn't lead me astray then I going to do as he has just asked. I'm going to leave room and shut all video surveillance off. If it is *you* in here Naida, I'm sorry about your friend. We are on our way back to the main land," Paul finished with only compassion in his voice.

Paul left the room leaving me feeling very alone and sad. After a few minutes had passed, Paul's lab coat began to ring. I felt my heart skip a beat; could it be? Would he be calling? I really longed for the warmth of his touch, his voice would be so soothing. I decided the thought of hearing his voice was more of a pull than if I were found out.

Pushing myself out of the water, my body took form. I stood on the platform surrounding Deuce's body. Hurrying over to the lab coat, I threw it around my body and dug into the pockets for the phone that continued to ring. I opened the lid to the phone as I had watched Paul earlier that day, and placed it on my ear.

"Hey Gills, are you there?" If my heart could dance, it would have been doing the foxtrot. It felt as though it would leave my chest if my ribs had not been holding it in place.

"Gills?" Cody's voice came again, but this time there was a little more concern in his tone.

"I'm here," my voice sounded much more quiet and small than I thought it should.

"Oh thank you…are you okay?" Cody said.

"I want to be with you," I stated. At the sound of his voice this time, it was as though I had woken up with a punch to my stomach. I hadn't realized how much I had missed Cody's touch and the strength which it gave me. I could almost see the smile on his beautiful face through the phone.

"I love you Gills. The ship is bringing you back now. I'll be waiting on the pier for you. My dad's gone to get you some more clothes. He'll be back in a few minutes with them. Just unlock the door when you're ready for him to come in."

"How much does your dad know?" I asked.

"Well, he knows he trusts me, but we are going to have to fill in the blanks." Cody let out a soft laugh. "Dad's okay; he'll wait until we're together before he really lets the questions fly. Don't worry."

"Okay so just unlock the door," I repeated.

"Yup, oh Gills? You *do* have the lab coat on right?" Cody's voice was so light we both let out a laugh together.

"Yes," I giggled.

"Good, I don't want my Dad getting a crush on you or anything. My Mom might get jealous, and besides which,…you're mine."

"No, you're mine," I replied as I walked up the stairs and turned the lock to release it. The doorknob turned slowly as if the person on the other side was concerned about an attack coming from my side of the door. Paul's head poked through the opening in the doorway.

"Here's some clothes. I hope they are okay. It's all I could find," Paul's voice was slow and stuttered.

"Thank you Paul. I'm sure they will be fine. Cody is on the line. Would you like to speak to him?" I asked.

"Sure".

"I'll see you soon. I love you," I said into the phone before handing it back to Paul.

Paul's head ducked back out the door allowing me some time to pull on the clothes he had found for me to wear. *Nice*, I thought, looking at the blue work coveralls. Fina would love these, I thought sarcastically. Oh well, it's better than trying to sneak off the ship naked, or wearing a lab coat; that would be difficult.

Paul snuck me into a small room just down from the one we were just in.
"Wait here. I will come get you when it is safe to get you off the ship without being noticed," Paul spoke in a hushed voice.

"Thank you, Paul," I said softly. He stopped before leaving and turned back to me.

"No Naida, it's me who should be thanking you. You've been a big help," Paul said.

"We've helped each other then," I said with a smile.

"Yes." And Paul left me alone in the tiny room to wait.

It looked like the room was an office of sorts though there was a tiny bed pushed into one corner of it. There were notes and books scattered all over the desk. A blue mug lay on the floor while a liquid, maybe that coffee stuff that Cody had bought for me once, was dripping off the edge of the desk. I sat down on the edge of the bed waiting, and noted some of the titles of the books that lay around me. Anatomy of the Killer Whale, Marine Biology Volume 1, Ocean Life—What lies beneath, and many other books. I decided I could be here a while so I stretched out on the bed and closed my eyes as I had seen Cody do on the beach before. It felt nice as the ship gently swayed back and forth. My body seemed to relax further until I was no long aware of where I was. My mind seemed to float through the most recent events, assessing and evaluating each situation. I thought of Cody walking towards Messina and I on the beach with his loving, warm eyes fixed on our *mostly* cold, hard eyes. The touch of his skin on mine as Messina left my body; this thought so warm, so comfortable now. It was like home, the place my soul belonged.

As I lay enjoying the thought of being with Cody, it was as though I could feel his warm lips pressing against my cheek. Then his breath in my ear, slowly and gently, "Gills?" As his finger brushed my cheek I realized, this wasn't just in my head. I opened my eyes with a flicker to see the eyes that I longed for. They were his eyes, so affectionately fixed on me, waiting for mine to join his.

"Hi," I said, with a bit of a lump now in my throat. I sat up and flung my arms around his neck while he put his arms around my waist, bringing me in close to his body. Neither of us said anything for several minutes. We just held on to each other as if we were afraid the other might slip away.

Finally, Cody broke the silence, "You never answered my question."

Not breaking the comfortable hold we had on each other I whispered into his ear, "What question was that?"

He continued the hold on me and breathed, "The one on the phone earlier, when I asked, 'Are you okay'?"

I felt my eyes fill with water, and it became difficult to see. The lump in my throat seemed to take up more space than I wanted it to, because when I went to speak, only a high-pitched noise seemed to escape my lips.

He ran one of his hands up my back and onto my head, gently stroking my hair, while my eyes continued to wet the shoulder of his shirt. My sobbing seemed to get harder as all the events appeared to come crashing in on top of me. Though we had beaten Messina, I had lost Deuce. The thought of his lifeless body in the room down the hall weighed heavy on me now. Even with his Mother's help it wasn't enough. If only I had been faster getting CoCo back to her family. The thoughts of 'If only'…continued running through my head. Cody could see I wasn't going to calm down anytime soon. So he decided to try, "Hey, you did everything you possibly could Naida. Stop please." Somehow I managed to find my voice, though the lump remained in my throat.

"I should have done more, he …," but that was all my voice would allow me to say. I broke into more sobs.

"Naida, you did more out there than any human could dream of doing. You helped in ways that many scientists only dream of. And it was only because of you that the two whales had a chance," Cody said in a strong and convincing tone.

"Deuce and Coco," I said softly.

"Pardon?" Cody looked puzzled.

"Deuce and Coco are the whales' names. Coco is the one we saved, Deuce is that one …" I lifted my arm to point in the direction of the other room where Deuce's body was.

"Of course. I'm sorry," Cody said.

Just then the door to the little room swung open and Paul entered, closing the door behind him. Cody stood up from the bed and helped me do the same.

"Hey, you kid's okay?" Paul asked, politely.

"Ah Dad, not a great question for Naida right now?" Cody said, still keeping one arm around my waist while we faced his father.

"Oh sorry," Paul said.

"It's okay, both of you. I'll be fine. It's just been…quite the day I guess," I said.

"We will need to get going. Oh, before we do though, Naida, would you like a minute with the whale before we leave the ship? They will be moving the body to the research lab at Dalhousie soon," Paul said.

"I'm okay, I said good-bye when he left his body," my eyes flicked up to Cody. "You would like to go and see the body, wouldn't you?" I said.

"Only if it wouldn't be too hard on you. I mean it's pretty amazing, really. They are such an awesome mammal that I have so much respect for," Cody replied.

"Is it okay if we go, Paul?" I said.

"Of course. Don't be too long though," Paul said.

"Thank you dad."

We followed Paul down the hall to the room. Paul decided not to come in with us. I walked down the stairs to the platform next to the body.

As I walked the length of Deuce's body, I ran my hand along his cold skin. He was so beautiful, so strong, and yet not strong enough to have overcome his fate. It was just then that I realized Cody wasn't beside me; I turned to find him still on the stairs of the entrance to the room.

"Cody what are you doing? Come here. I thought you wanted to see Deuce's body," I said.

"I did. I just didn't think it would hurt so much. I mean, I felt your pain but just seeing him there just . . ." a steady stream of tears was making Cody's face shine.

I smiled at Cody. "Come here," I said again. This time I walked to the foot of the stairs, and held out my hand for Cody to take. He came down and placed his hand in mine as we walked over to the huge body lying in a pool of water. I took Cody's hand and placed it on the nose of Deuce's body. I then placed my hand over top of his.

"Cody, it's okay. I'm okay, and these are some of the reasons why I'm here," I said, and let my hand drop but Cody left his on Deuce's nose.

"He's so big. I wish I could communicate with them the way you do," Cody said, continuing to walk along side Deuce. He was taking the time to examine, not only the feel of his skin, but the indents and marks time had left on Deuce's majestic body.

"You can communicate with their kind, through me. I think this is the start of something very positive for my ocean," I said.

"Are you guys ready?" Paul's voice came from the top of the stairs.

"Sure Dad. Thanks," Cody answered his dad in a low voice.

We followed Paul out to the pier. When we were out of view of anyone that may have been watching us come off the ship, the three of us came to a stop.

"I'll see you at home then?" Paul said to Cody and I.

"Sure Dad, I'll take Naida back to her Mother and meet you at the house," Cody said.

"That is not entirely what I meant. Naida, I think we need to have a chat." Paul raised his eyebrow and look at me, knowing we all knew what the topic of conversation would be.

"Yes. I know Mother would like you to join us for a discussion. If everyone is up to it, we could do it tonight." I thought we might as well get this conversation over with. Paul had been so good about dealing with so much on very little information. I couldn't imagine the talk would be too difficult for him to digest. He had to have so many questions, and so much on his mind.

"Okay, so Naida's place it is then. Do you have your car down here dad?" Cody asked.

"Yes but I would like to grab dinner and a shower before I come over. Do you think your Mother would be okay with doing it in a couple of hours or so?" Paul asked.

"That's fine Paul; she will be happy to have you whenever you're ready," I said.

"How about around 8:00 tonight, Dad? Do you know where their cottage is?" Cody gave his dad direction and we said good–bye, and made our way to Cody's car. I had no idea what time it was, or what day it was for that matter. Time seemed to have been standing still since I hit the water after the spill.

"How long has it been since the spill, Cody?" I asked.

TIDES

"4 days; you don't remember?" Cody said.

"No, when I'm in the water I don't pay attention to how many times the sun goes up and down. On land it's easier to keep track, but down below the surface, it's much harder," I said. By the time we reached his car, Cody was a couple steps ahead of me. He opened the passenger door and held it for me to get in. Watching me as I got in, he let out a smooth chuckle, "I realize I have my dad to thank for this, but those coveralls you're wearing sure look hot."

I looked down, having forgotten all about what I was wearing.

"Oh yeah, thanks. I thought they matched the blue in my *eyes*. I'm so glad you like them. Maybe if you play your cards right I'll get you a matching pair." I laughed, and threw a wink at him as he closed my car door.

We were back to the little cottage within minutes. Mother, Fina, Aella and Chief Grey Feather were waiting for us on the beach by the fire. Aella was first to welcome us back.

"Hey Naida, Cody. Over here!" Aella called to us.

As we got closer I could see everyone one was smiling and happy with our return. Mother's eyes looked watery as if she had been crying, but she quickly wiped them clear, and joined the welcoming committee.

"Naida," Mother said, as she put her hands on my shoulders and pulled me into her chest. She held me tightly for only a few seconds, and with a huge sigh, she released me.

Fina danced over and gave me huge, "I'm glad you're back, Naida." It was all she said, but I knew it meant a great deal. Then Aella came over and hugged me; her hug was much more natural then Fina's, though I knew they were both equal in meaning. As Aella let go of me, my eyes came to rest on the Chief, and with a nod of his head, he gestured for all of us to sit down around the fire. Cody took the seat next to me, slipping his arm around my back to pull me in so our hips were touching, while his hand sat warmly on my other hip.

"You and Cody have done well together over the past couple of days. I'm proud of both of you," as he said this the Chief nodded his head at Cody and I again. "It appears that you and Cody were up for the test and passed it with few casualties. Very good." The Chief sounded pleased.

"Casualties! I can't stay. I need to talk to CoCo and her family," I blurted out. As I jumped to my feet to leave, Cody caught my arm in his hand.

My eyes flicked from Cody to Aella and she was the one to speak now, "While you were on the ship Mother sent me out to deliver the news to Deuce's family. I caught up with them on the outer limits of the spill. They were there waiting for you and Deuce to return. CoCo was very upset. I take it they were very close. The rest of his family seemed to take it in stride, though his Mother became very quiet at the sound of the news. They all wanted me to thank you for all your efforts and wished you a safe return. I'm sorry Naida, I know you would have wanted to have been the one to tell them, but we didn't want them to be waiting any longer than they already had been." Aella looked so apologetic as she filled me in. I felt nothing but sorrow for Deuce's family.

I took my seat beside Cody again and said, "Thank you Aella, perhaps I will cross paths with the family again sometime."

"I understand we are to expect a visitor this evening." Mother said softly. I was now wondering how much she had been visiting my thoughts since all this started.

"Yes, he will be here around 8, but you probably already know that, don't you?" I said a little sarcastically.

"Now Naida, I haven't been in your thoughts more than necessary. And I have made you aware that I'm listening almost every time. Now that things have settled, I won't need to do it as much," Mother said, not sounding too apologetic.

"No, I'm sorry. If you hadn't been listening, then Cody may have believed Messina, and I may have lost everything to her," I said.

"Ah, but we are a team, and together with truths being told, we can beat anything. Messina didn't understand the team in which you are apart," Mother said calmly.

"You are very strong together," Cody said supporting Mother's claim. However, Mother's expression changed to one of concern as her eyes fell onto Cody alone.

"You're not quite there yet are you? I mean to say you haven't quite understood the importance of your role to the survival of all of us. You are a very important part of our *team*. Your understanding of how you can protect and preserve all of us is growing, but maybe the concept is too great yet for you to entirely grasp. If you act with as much love in your heart as you did on the beach to save Naida, in everything you do, then the earth will flourish with your love." Mother's voice was strong and committed to the intention of her words. The Chief seemed to be surveying the expressions on all of our faces, but in particular, Cody's. Several moments passed while most of us just watched the flames dancing in the fire.

The Chief cleared his throat to speak, "There will come a time that each one of you will need to bond with your human soul mate. In Cody and Naida's case, the bond has been strong from the beginning, and Cody's soul has been clear to accept so much in such a short period of time. I hope as time passes each of your unions can be as natural as this one."

Night was falling, and as it did, Fina twitched in her seat until Mother finally said, "Fina. Aella. Go and join your sources for the night. Cody's father will be here soon and your presence is not required for that. The fewer there are of us here, the more comfortable it will make it for Paul."

Fina let out a thankful sigh and got to her feet. Aella, on the other hand, stood and looked at Mother. "Are you sure?" she asked. "I'm okay to stay if you need me at all."

Fina was already half way into the fire when she paused to hear Mother's reply, "No. You two go and get refreshed. Who knows what tomorrow might hold for us," she said causing all the focus to shift to her, while she just flung her head back and let out a chuckle.

Fina gave a crooked little smile as she disappeared into the fire. With Fina's sense for drama, I could only imagine that most of her pay cheques from the club were going to buy new clothes as so many had gone up in flames.

Aella was never quite as dramatic as Fina about her union with her source. She just walked over to the trees by the water, and within a blink her clothing sat on the sand to await her return. I got up, walked over, folded her clothes and left them on the rock for her.

As I walked back I caught sight of a lone figure walking down the hill towards the fire.

"Cody. Your Dad is here," I said. Cody, Mother and the Chief all stood, while Cody headed over to meet his Dad on the beach.

"Hey, you found us." Cody called over to his Dad.

"Yeah, no problem. Good directions, kiddo." Paul's voice was light. When Cody reached his Dad, Paul put his hand on his shoulder and gave it a squeeze. Paul said something to his son in a low voice that the three of us by the fire couldn't make out, but whatever it was, Cody just threw his head back and laughed. When they got close enough I could see Paul's face was warm and gentle.

Cody did the introductions: "Anna Terra; this is my dad, Paul Angel."

"Hello Paul. Welcome," Mother said.

"And this is Chief Grey Feather. Chief, this is my dad."

"Welcome," the Chief also replied.

"Thank you. Hello Naida. How are you feeling?"

"Okay Paul. Thank you for joining us tonight."

"It looks like you're growing fond of those coveralls. Careful, or you might start a trend."

I laughed, because I had completely forgotten that I was still in my borrowed clothes. "Yes, well, I won't tell you what your son thinks of them."

"I can only imagine". Paul gave his son a rather crooked smile.

Mother invited everyone to sit. She began with, "Paul may I get you something to drink? Cody what was that stuff I have in the cottage for you?"

"It's called Gingerale," Cody answered Mother with a light chuckle.

"Right. So we have that, or some wine that Fina brought home the other day. She said it sells well at the Club and we should try it," Mother noted.
"Well, if you're opening the wine, that sounds fine to me," Paul said.

"Mother; Cody and I can go and get it. It'll give me a chance to change into something more comfortable, and Cody can open the wine. How many glasses should I get?" I asked.

"Get 5; we can all try it. I'm sure Fina won't mind. I'd ask her, but I don't think she is really listening," Mother said as the 4 of us laughed and Paul looked as though he missed the joke.

"My sisters just left Paul. You'll have to meet them next time," I said.

"I'd like that," he smiled politely.

Cody and I made our way back to the cottage. While he rummaged for some glasses, I slipped out of the coveralls into my sweat pants and Dalhousie sweat top. I made my way back out to the kitchen area. Cody was working on opening the bottle.

"Humph," Cody said as he caught sight of me.

"What?" I said, a little disappointed with the sound he just made.

A mischievous smile broke over his lips as he said, "I was hoping you'd need some help with those coveralls." He reached over and pulled me into his arms. My next breath was full of him; a scent I had missed so much for the past few weeks, that I probably over did it. I filled my lungs as full as they could go, and I felt my head spin a bit, but I didn't care. I just closed my eyes and enjoyed. I was back where I wanted to be. His arms just felt like a familiar warm blanket, one that the cold couldn't penetrate.

I realized that he was doing the same thing I was. His nose was tucked in my hair at the top of my head and he too, was just breathing.

I opened my eyes to see the wine perched on the counter with 5 glasses beside it. It took me a minute, but then it clicked in as to why we were inside, and what we were supposed to be doing.

"Well, we should get back out there before Mother freaks your dad out too much," I said with a giggle.

"I don't like to say it, but you're probably right," said Cody as he picked up the wine and some of the glasses while I grabbed the rest. We joined the others outside by the fire. Cody poured the wine and handed everyone a glass.

Chief Grey Feather raised his glass and said, "I believe this is how a toast is done. Here is to a strong, long lasting relationship." Everyone clinked glasses and took a sip of wine.

Mother held the wine in her mouth a while before swallowing hers. She then said, "Very good. Those are French grapes."

"Ah, you're right. Good one, Anna," Cody said examining and bottle, "How did you know?"

Mother cocked her head to the side and raised one eyebrow at him. "Cody, do you really need to ask? Let me just say I know my grapes." She smiled and he seemed to understand.

"Well Paul; it is okay that I call you Paul, isn't it?" Mother began.

"Of course, if I may call you Anna." Paul replied.

"Agreed. Well Paul, I would like to keep this conversation as honest and open as possible. No *secrets*. However, I think it best if we answer your questions, as opposed to overwhelming you with too much information. Do you agree?" Mother asked.

"Yes, that sounds fine. I'm not sure I know where to begin though. I have so many questions running around in my head." Paul paused for a moment, but it didn't take him long to bring on the first question.

"This may sound like an odd question to begin with, knowing all that I could start with, but why Cody? Why has Naida chosen to be with my son?" Paul finished, looking a little embarrassed.

A smile turned up the corners of Mother's mouth, as she responded, "Not at all an odd question, and one that really speaks to the heart of the matter. I appreciate your question, and if he were my son I to would want to address that one also." Mother took a deep breath and began, "Your son and Naida have a bond, one that extends beyond that of physical beings. He is in love with all that she is and she is in love with all that he is. He, unlike most humans, can see beyond what Naida presents as her physical self. Cody has always known Naida, and has always been able to see her, even when she was in her water form." Mother glanced over at Cody for a moment before continuing, "I guess that is, with the exception of the short period of time that he had talked himself out of seeing her." She smiled and got back on topic. "This bond is very important, however, right now the bond is more crucial than it his ever been. This is why Naida has taken a physical form, so she can strengthen and nourish it, so it may flourish."

Paul took a minute to digest the information and then regrouped with the next one, "What is Naida then?" Though his questions were short in words, they were deep in meaning.

"May I answer this one Anna?" Chief Grey Feather responded before Mother could open her mouth.

"Yes, please," Mother said.

"Thank you. You see Paul, many, many years ago, the ocean was in harmony; there was a balance. The creatures of the oceans respected the laws of nature, and though there were predators and prey, there existed a balance between them, and from that balance a love was born into our waters. This love was a respect that the creatures had for one another. The prey knew of its purpose, as the predators of theirs, and as in the circle of life, the predators were also prey. This love that was born, traveled the waters, growing strong from the harmony around her. Centuries passed and this love watched the evolution of the creatures within her birthplace. The balance and harmony has continued, until recently. By recently I mean, within the last 50 to 100 years. Though humans do not live in the ocean, they impact the harmony within the waters. Their methods of fishing and technology are pushing the harmony, causing it to become unbalanced. This destruction should never been confused with evolution. Naida is the ocean's love and these changes are killing her, *slowly*, but killing her all the same." The Chief sat back scanning Paul's face.

Paul seamed to take it in stride, just as his son had when things were explained to him. Paul sat quietly for a moment taking another sip of wine from his glass. As he pulled it away from his mouth, he analyzed the liquid in the glass as though it were the first time he had ever seen anything like it before. Then his eyes moved from the glass to me, and as I stared back into his eyes, a smile seemed to warm his face, and I knew he was digesting the information favorably. I was coming into focus for another member of the Angel family.

Paul took another sip and breathed in deeply before releasing another question, "Okay Cody, I guess my next question is for you. Are you okay with all of this?"

Cody smiled at his dad. "Well Dad, this is probably going to be the shortest answer you get tonight, but *Yes* from the bottom of my soul I'm okay with this." Cody answered his Dad with more conviction in his voice than I have ever heard from anyone before.

Paul turned to face me, "You can communicate with everything in the ocean?"

"Yes Paul, I do more than just communicate with them, I'm a part of all of them." Paul's face was serious as if the concept were stretching his mind to new places.

"The logical scientific side of me would like to say I don't believe you, or that I don't understand, but for some reason that side of me is being hushed because I know what you say is true. I guess my scientific side would like to know *how,* though that isn't really what's important," Paul said.

"Perhaps I should just show you, Paul," I said as Cody let out a soft gulp of air. As I stood, I held out my hand for Paul to take. He stood and accepted my hand. Once we reached the shoreline I gave Paul a second to kick off his shoes. I knew I could now control the union of my source, so we walked slowly into the water.

I turned to Paul when we were about knee deep in the salty water. I took his other hand in mine, "Watch me carefully okay?" and as he nodded at me, I allowed myself to join my source, dissolving out of his hands like the salt within the water where we stood.

"Naida?" Paul called out.

"It's okay Dad, she's right there by your feet," Cody was standing in the water just behind his Dad now, likely preparing for his reaction in case it wasn't a favorable one.

"You can still see her?" Paul sounded surprised.

"Yes and she is just as beautiful in the water, as out," Cody smiled knowing I could of course still hear him.

I moved over to the trees to get out where Mother was waiting with some dry clothes. "Thanks Mother, it's going well isn't it?" I said as I pulled them on out of sight and sound of Paul and the others.

"I think so, but only time will truly tell," Mother said.

By the time Mother and I got back over to the fire, Paul and Cody were there with Chief Grey Feather finishing their wine.

The look on Paul's face frightened me a bit. It was very serious, confused, and there was something else that I couldn't put my finger on. "I think I've had enough for tonight, if that's alright? Thank you Anna for your hospitality. Chief it was nice to meet you, and Naida …" Paul took a long pause before he continued. "Naida, you must understand I have always had science and facts to back everything I know to be true. Tonight's information is forcing me to use a side of my brain that I've fallen out of touch with. Let me sleep on it and I assure you all, what is said in this circle will stay in this circle. Cody, may I speak to you a moment please?"

Paul stood and so did the rest of us. Mother took his glass and thanked him for coming, "We can do this again when you're ready."

"Sure, thank you all. Good Night," Paul said as he left the fire with Cody.
Cody was only gone a couple of minutes when he returned to the fire and he and I sat again. However, Mother and the Chief stayed standing.

"I think we will get out of your hair now kids. Cody, will you be staying late?" Mother asked.

He smiled, "My dad just asked the same question. He knows I've missed a lot of school and should get back to it tomorrow. I'll likely stay a few hours." Cody's arm was around me and it pleased me to hear he would stay for a bit. Mother and the Chief nodded and said good night. The two stepped back into the darkness where the light from the fire could no longer touch them.

"Come on, let's move down the beach a bit. Fina is still in the fire, and I would like to be alone with you right now," I said giving Cody what was intended to be a very sexy smile, though I'm not sure I did it right, 'cause he just seemed to laugh a little.

We found a place just down from the cottage near the cluster of trees. The sound of the waves crashing onto shore was rhythmic and relaxing. They weren't angry waves just waves, the way I liked them.

CHAPTER 16

What's Normal?

Cody sat down on the sand and stretched his legs out in front of him. I sat down beside him and turned so I could drape my legs over his while wrapping my arms around his torso. My head rested on his chest.

"Was your dad okay when he left?" I asked.

"Yeah, he's just so left brained that stuff like this is tough for him. He'll come around, and watch out, when he does, you'll be pelted with questions," Cody said, yawning at the end.

"Hey. You need to get some sleep; you have a big day at school tomorrow with all the catching up you have to do," I said.

"I think I have more catching up to do with you, than with school right now." He lay back onto the sand and pulled me with him. I ended up with my body pressing against his, nose to nose, and eyes fixed on each other.

"You know Gills, it's always hard to let you go in the water, but that last time had to be the hardest. Hey, we need to be a regular couple for an evening. How about I take you out tomorrow night? School is done at four tomorrow, and I can pick you up around five or six. It's a Friday night, so I'll have the weekend to clean up any homework I need to catch up on," Cody said.

"Okay, but no movie. Let's do something different," I said.

"Sure, Let me look into a couple things. I have a few ideas but I need to get the details first."

"Okay. Well, what else do normal couples do?" I asked, giving him a very coy smile.

"Well a little bit of this …" Cody moved in to press his lips on my neck, which sent a shiver down my spine. I had missed that feeling so much.
"And maybe some of this …" I pulled my head back and lined my lips up with his, as I pressed them into his, a warmth consumed my body from head to toe.

"Yeah, that feels pretty *normal*," Cody said when we parted from our kiss.
I rolled over and sat up, "I can't imagine a life without you now."

Cody sat up too, "Well that's okay Gills, 'cause I'm not going anywhere."
"… but what if I do?" I questioned. "What if there's another Messina, what if the trawlers never stop?" Suddenly my warm mood switched to one of sadness.

"If that happens Gills, then this world is not going to be to great for anyone, and that is not an option. We are an awesome team and now that I have found you again, I'm not going to let you go. I'm going to fight for everything you and we are together." Cody's warm eyes and inviting smile seemed to make the biggest concern seem like nothing. I *did* feel like we could repair the damage together.

"So I guess you really are my *boyfriend* then?" I said with a giggle. The title 'boyfriend' seemed so small compared to what Cody really was to me.

"Yeah, if this is a boyfriend to you, then I'd hate to see what a husband is. Actually…hum." Cody's face went from playful to thoughtful, and then to yawn.

"You need to get home. Come on. I'll walk you up to your car," I said, and stood up and put my hands out to pull him to his feet.

"Thanks Gills, I guess I am pretty tired. You sure make for an exciting time. Are you going back out tonight?" Cody asked.
"Yeah, I think I will for a bit. Especially if my boyfriend is taking me out tomorrow night." I smiled at him as we started up the hill towards his car. "Besides, how else would I pass the time. You're going to be in school, and work still thinks I'm sick."

"Right. Well I'll be back around 6:00 pm tomorrow night to take out on a *normal* date," Cody said.

"Good, I'll be ready and you get some sleep. I love you," I said.

"I love you too Gills." Cody put his arms around my waist and pulled me into body. I wished the kiss he gave me next could have lasted the night, but I think he might have fallen asleep if it had lasted any longer than it did.
As he went to get into his car I called over, "Drive carefully!"

"See you tomorrow Gills."

As he drove away I turned and made my way back to my ocean.

I joined my ocean for the remainder of the evening. It was a quiet evening, though I had found evidence of the deep ocean trawler having been through again. Nothing else seemed to be out of place. After a while I heard Aella on the surface calling me.

"Naida?"

"Hey, how has your evening been in the skies?" I said as I crested the surface.

"Wonderful, how was yours?" Aella replied.

"It was good. Mother says only time will truly tell how Paul will deal with the information though. For now I'm just glad I'm able to see Cody again, and that our first test is over with." I said.

"Hey did you hear the Chief tonight saying that all of us have someone we are bonded to. Do you think there is a "Cody" out there for me?" Aella said.

"Perhaps, and if there is, I hope he is as wonderful as mine," I said. Aella and I sailed around the ocean, her on top and me underneath, for hours, each of us storing our energy from our sources. As the morning broke, Aella said she needed to get back in so she and Fina could make it into work on time.

The two of us made for the cottage on the beach. I walked Aella up to the cottage and we entered together. When we walked in Mother and Fina were just ending an argument though neither, Aella nor I heard what it was about. Mother's cheeks were flush from the nature of the conversation. It only took her a moment, to recover, and she was happy fresh Mother again.

"We will need to let the Beach Club know that you are well again, so you can return to work," Mother said.

"Mother do you think that is the best place for me in which to integrate, now that I have found Cody? I mean, maybe I should be at

Dalhousie with him, shouldn't I? After watching so many of the students on the ship working on CoCo and preparing to work on Deuce, maybe that's where I really should be," I said, hoping that she would buy into my idea. Even in my own mind, though, I wasn't sure if it was more about spending time with Cody.

"Yes, I had thought of that too, Naida. I would like to see how Paul is with the information before we go pushing you on him anymore than we already have been doing. It is very important that he is fully on board with all that you are. Hopefully he will see how helpful you can be to him, and of course him to you. No, for now I think we should just get you back into work at the beach club, and wait and see how Paul reacts. Aella, would you let Mrs. Snorff know that your sister is better, and can likely return to work on Monday."

"Sure Mother. I will do that first thing."

After my sisters left for work, Mother and I sat talking for a while. Mostly about the spill; I wasn't sure if Mother was avoiding the topic of Messina or not, but I was glad we didn't have to go there. The thought of her and the threat she posed still left me cold and scared.

Finally Mother stood up and said, "Well if you don't mind dear, I'm going to be with my source. There are a few things I need to check on. Are you going to be okay for the day?"

"Oh of course Mother, please go. I'll likely just hang around here for a bit, and Cody and I have a date tonight, so don't rush, I'll be fine. Actually, would you mind if I went and got some clothes for tonight? I'll just walk into downtown Lunenburg and have a look through some of the shops there."

"Sounds like a great idea. Here, take some money," Mother said as she handed me a fist full of small bills from the cupboard, gave me a hug, and walked out the door.

I poked my head out the door after her, "Mother is everything alright?"

"Yes dear. Your sister just stirred up a little trouble last night that I need to tend to; not to worry. Enjoy your day," Mother smiled and shot me a wink. She kicked off her shoes and her body began to spin. Within seconds Mother's physical body had dissolved into the sand. She was with her source now.

I walked out, gathered her clothes and placed them just inside the door of the cottage. A couple hours later I was walking down the main street of Lunenburg looking in all the shop windows. I had no idea what I was looking for. I was just killing time until I could be with Cody again.

Finally I arrived at one shop that looked promising. As I walked in, a little bell rung above my head, and a lady seemed to pop out of nowhere.

"Oh hello dear. May I help you?" she said, scanning me from top to bottom.

"Thank you. I just thought I would look around if that's alright?" I said softly.

"Certainly. Let me know if I can help," she said as she turned and started to fuss with some clothes on a rack near to her. After peeling through three or four racks, I found the top three outfits I liked, and went to try them on. After trying on the second, the lady decided to see if she could help again.

"May I ask, is this for a particular evening, dear?"

"No. Well, yes. Just, my boyfriend is taking me out tonight and I want to look nice, maybe…even *hot*, but definitely not puffy or frilly," I said, now a flushed in the cheeks.

"Wonderful, let me try something. What size are you?"

TIDES

...

About an hour later I was on my way home with my new purchase in tow, and feeling very proud of my selection. It was then that a smell caught my nose. My head started to spin, and I felt like I would throw up if I didn't get away from the odor. I looked up at the building where the stench seemed to be coming from. Several men and women in suits were all sitting in the window eating. I moved my eyes to the sign on the building: *Chuck's Seafood Café*. Ugh. No wonder, I probably knew half the entrees.

The people in the windows were laughing and eating, barely looking at their food as they shoved more in. Mouthful after mouthful, until they looked as though they might explode. I watched a woman walk over and take some plates off the table. The food still piled on the plates, but the patrons just waving their hands as if to say "No more". I saw some uneaten shellfish on the one plate and I realized I couldn't take any more.

Walk just walk, I kept on telling myself as I hurried away from the smell. Soon I was out of the range of the smell and was able to focus and clear my head again.

I was back home in no time and began pulling the tags off my new outfit. I looked up at the clock. Four and a half more hours until Cody would be back. I decided it was enough time for a quick swim, and then I could get ready for our date. Boy did I ever hope he wasn't planning on taking me to Chuck's tonight.

The time still seemed to be on slow motion setting. When I got out of the water, I thought it had to be close to 5:00 pm, but as it turned out, I had been in the water for less than 2 hours. *Pathetic*, I thought to myself.

I decided to try something that seemed very human. I pulled on some clothes, and turned on the TV that Mother had bought. TV seemed so weird, coupled with the fact that every channel seemed as if it were in a snowstorm of sort. One channel had some funny looking people running around singing odd-sounding songs. I think it was intended for young humans, but the snow affect that my TV gave the show actually made it funny to me. The next channel had a huge fire blazing in a forest just north west of us. A man stood holding a stick with a ball on the end of it, speaking into the TV. He was explaining how no one was able to tell how the fire was started, but that firefighters were working tirelessly to try to get it under control. I watched, as the trees seemed to turn from beautiful healthy statues, to lifeless, burnt, fallen-over pieces of ash and ruin. I wondered if the humans felt the same way about forest fires as they do about oil spills in my ocean. Hmmm?

Finally enough time passed, and that everyone started coming home. Aella and Fina walked in while I was still watching the TV. I found it to be rather mind-numbing, but it passed the time, all the same.

"Have you seen Mother?" Fina asked, almost cautiously.

"No. She left this morning after you guys took off to work. Hey! What time is it?" I asked as I looked up at the clock. 5:15. Good. That would give me enough time to get ready.

"Why? What are you up to tonight?" Aella asked.

"Cody and I are going on a date. Come here. I bought some new clothes and I want you to see them." I grabbed Aella's hand and pulled her upstairs to our room where the pile of new clothes sat neatly folded on the edge of the bed. Fina however didn't share my excitement; she just sat down in the chair in the kitchen and stared at the little TV though. It didn't look as though she was really looking at the TV picture at all.

"So where is he taking you?" Aella pressed.

"I don't know. It sounded like he wanted to have a *normal* date. Whatever that means," I said.

"Well, come on then. Put your new stuff on so I can see, before he gets here and steals you away. Were you in the ocean today? How was the water? Calmer I hope," Aella smiled.

"Calmer, yes, but not much happier. Even though Messina is gone, there's still a sense of sadness in the water. It was such a happier time when the humans only took what they needed. Now they waste so many creatures. The others in the waters know it, and I can feel their sorrow," I said and took a deep breath. When I looked back at Aella she reached out and wiped a tear from my eye.

"Hey. No, no, no, Naida. Tonight is a happy night…just let go and enjoy for one night. Please, Naida you need it. Look at you. That outfit is amazing and you know what?" Aella said as she stood up and called down to Fina. "Hey Fina, can Naida wear that necklace you were wearing the other night? It would look perfect with her new outfit."

We were waiting for her reply, and when one didn't come, we realized there was a fire in the fireplace and Fina's clothes lay on the floor beside it. "Well I'm sure she won't mind." Aella said as she removed the necklace from a hook beside Fina's bed. "Here hold still", she said, while slipping around my neck, a pretty silver necklace with an ornate looking square pendant on it.

"Wow, I really like it. Where did Fina get it, Aella?"
"Not too sure, it caught my eye the other night, but I forgot to ask her," Aella said with a look on her face as though she was trying to remember why she hadn't asked Fina. Finally Aella did a little shrug and looked back at me with her warm smile. "I'm so glad you're safe. That Messina was some creation."

"Yeah,…Aella. Has mother mentioned anything to you about Messina, and if it could happen again?" I asked with a look of concern on my face.

"I can't say we really looked at it from that angle. While you were dealing with her, Mother was focused on your thoughts and helping you. Can't say we discussed any of that. Why?"

"Well, I thought once Messina was gone, there would be a universal ease throughout the water. But on the contrary; it's like everything is waiting for something now. By getting rid of Messina, I feel like I was only getting rid of a symptom, which was only a result of a much larger illness within my water. Now it feels like everyone just waits."

With a huge sigh, Aella placed both hands on either side of my face. "Oh Naida please…let yourself go for one night. Cody will be here soon and you need an evening to enjoy one another, without the weight of all of mankind, and the salvation of our earth on your shoulders," Aella finished with both a creased up forehead, and a half smile on her face, obviously doubting I could do as she asked.

"I know…you're right, but …" just as I went to finish my sentence, there was a knock at the door, and the most warm and inviting voice with it.

"Hey Gills, you inside?" Cody called out.

My stomach seemed to do a flip at the sound of his voice, and as I went to answer, it was like my mouth had gone dry and the words wouldn't come.

Finally Aella said, "Come on in Cody, she'll just be a minute."

We heard the cottage door open and close. "Thanks Aella. Is everything okay?" Cody said.

"Oh yeah, Naida 's just happy to hear you, that's all." Aella said, giving a little chuckle as she walked down the stairs to where Cody stood.

TIDES

I fixed my outfit one last time, and hurried down to see Cody. As I reached the bottom of the stairs, I could smell the familiar scent of Cody's cologne. I loved that smell. As soon as my feet left the stairs and hit the floor, Cody's eyes moved from Aella, to whom he was still talking, on to me.

The smile that I longed to see was instantly on his lips; his eyes were soft and warm. I hurried over to his waiting arms and once they securely surrounded me, I felt my heart give a pang of comfort to know I was complete once more.

"So Gills; you ready for a fun night?" Cody said gently into my ear.

"Well, I guess that depends on what you call fun," I replied with a giggle.

"We'll be able to get into lots of trouble with that outfit; you look great, Gills."

Cody pulled me away from his body, still keeping a relaxed grip on my shoulders, all the while surveying my entire *landscape*. His eyes seemed to record every inch of me.

"I take it you like it, then. The saleswoman seemed to think you might," I said.

"Well it looks like that saleswoman is very good at her job," Cody said, still looking very intently at me.

Aella cleared her throat, "I think I'll get going now. Naida is on firm orders that she is only to have fun tonight…and by the look in your eye Cody, it looks as though you can handle that, so I'll see you tomorrow."

"Okay Aella, enjoy," I said, still not taking my eyes off Cody.

"You too," Aella said, shutting the cottage door behind her.

"We should get going too, if we're going to make our reservations," Cody said looking at his watch.

But just as we started to move towards the door, Mother burst through it into the little cottage. She looked as though she was going to rip something, or someone, apart, but before anyone could speak, her expression softened.

"Oh, it's you two. Going out for the evening, are you? Well have a fun time," Mother sounded as though she were dismissing us, and with the previous look on her face, I was all to happy to be dismissed.

"Yes Mother, Thank you," I said and Cody and I took our leave.

Cody had picked up on the mood change too and wasted no time getting me into his car. The car started on the second try and we were off. We didn't drive very long before we were in a small hamlet just outside of Lunenburg. It was a beautiful little spot, but it didn't look big enough to support a restaurant. Cody seemed pretty sure of himself though, so I didn't interrupt his mood with my uncertainty.

As we drove along a tiny single lane road, I sensed that these old homes on either side of the tiny road had my ocean in their backyards, though with nightfall it had gotten too shadowy and hard to see. At the end of the road sat an old but beautiful two-story home. It had a very inviting feel to it, though I couldn't have told you why. Just a feeling, or perhaps a feeling I got from Cody. Perhaps he was comfortable here.

We pulled into the driveway and a smile broke across Cody's gentle face. "We're here," his voice sang out as he leaped from the car shutting his door behind him. Before I could reach for the door handle, Cody was pulling the door open and offering me a hand out.

"Thank you Cody…but where are we, it feels so …" My voice trailed off as my eyes came to rest on a woman standing in the archway of the front door the house. She appeared to be the reason for the comfort that the home seemed to radiate. A smile broke over her face, pushing her checks up, which seemed to move her half moon glasses up on her nose. She opened her arms and warmly called out to Cody and I: "Oh, welcome kids, come on in."

As Cody and I walked up the front steps, the woman took a step back into the house. As we entered, I was warmly greeted with the smell of apple pie and cinnamon. However, I could still make out the smell of my ocean underneath all of the other scents. As Cody and I walked through the entrance, the woman grabbed Cody around the waist and gave him a hug.

Cody cleared his throat and said, "Naida this is a very special woman in my life. This is Mrs. Victoria Angel."

Just then the woman laughed and released Cody. She reached for me and said, "...but you can call me Grandma, dear." As the little woman hugged me, I couldn't help but smile.

CHAPTER 17

Apple Pie With a Side of Memories

"Grandma Angel. You're Cody's Grandma. It's so nice to meet you." Her hug felt warm and comforting. We followed Grandma further into the house. I glanced at all the old and new pictures of what appeared to be loved ones. On shelves and mantels, on tables and walls, the house was filled with smiling faces peering out of picture frames. One man's face was in many of the pictures; some just of him standing alone with a uniform on.

Just then I saw it; it was like a spark to a wick. The same man that was in many of the pictures was there in the centre of the mantel in a beautiful gold and black frame. He sat posing on the bow of a fishing boat, with a bright smile and one hand holding some thick ropes. I walked over to the picture forgetting I was supposed to be following Cody and his Grandma. I stopped at the fireplace and picked up the picture to get a better look. I knew this man, very well. Before I could stop myself, tears began to well up in my eyes, making it harder and harder to see the man in the picture.

A voice called out "Gills, where did you go?" Cody popped his head back in the room. "Hey what are you doing still in here? Grandma and ..." but his voice stopped short as he caught the look on my face and the picture I was holding. I just looked from Cody to the picture and back again.

Just then Grandma came back into the room too. "Is everything alright dears?" She saw me standing by the fireplace with the picture in both hands, and tears streaming down my face. "Oh dear," Cody's Grandma began, "are you alright?" She paused for a moment and looked more intensely at me. "Did you know my husband, dear?"

Of course. This was a picture of Grandpa Angel; I loved this man. In a very small voice I said, "Yes, he was a great Man."

A smile broke over Grandma Angel's face, one of pride and love for the man of whom I was speaking with such admiration. Grandma's face was soft and warm, "I would like to hear about how you knew my husband, but first, please join me in the kitchen. We can talk over dinner."

I wiped the tears from my eyes and gently placed the picture back on the mantel, and followed her into the kitchen. As I walked, Cody slipped his arm around my shoulder and bent into my ear. "My Grandma will understand. You can speak openly with her. She is very…accepting of these things."

We entered the beautiful country kitchen, with a big oak table, which was set in a windowed breakfast nook. The windows looked out on a point; my ocean was all you could see. It was so beautiful. I stopped at the table and stared at the wonder of my ocean. It was quiet for a moment or two until I realized both Cody and his Grandma were both just looking at me as I stood admiring the breathtaking view.

I felt Grandma at my shoulder, "This was his favorite place in the house," she said quietly, "near the end, he would just sit here and stare out, hour after hour. No one would dare to move him. At first the view seemed to bring him comfort, but after several weeks of it, his face looked more and more troubled. I have no idea what he was thinking about 'cause he didn't have the strength to speak. The ocean used to bring him such peace, but as I say, near the end it was like…it was a worry to him."

I turned to look into Grandma's eyes. She appeared to be lost in her thoughts now. I placed my hand on her shoulder, and her eyes seemed to come back into focus. "Perhaps he was worried," I said quietly.

Grandma just smiled and invited me to sit at the table. "Here dear, why don't you sit here." She offered me a seat that faced the big window. Cody pulled out the chair and waited for me to sit. Then he helped his Grandma put all the food on the table before pulling out the seat to my left for his grandma to sit in.

Finally he took his place on my right and gave my shoulder a gentle squeeze before sitting down. "Grandma you've out done yourself once again!" Cody said.

"Yes Grandma Angel, everything looks so good," I said appreciatively. She closed her eyes for a moment or two, and a smile broke over her lips as though she were sharing something special in her head.

Her eyes fluttered back open and she said, "Please help yourselves, kids." Cody didn't need to be told twice. He started filling his plate and passing the bowls around the table. The conversation over dinner was kept light as I got to know Grandma more, and she got to know me. Cody would laugh under his breath as I would brush over many of the details of my life to Grandma in an attempt to keep things light.

After dinner Grandma offered us tea with our pie, and both Cody and I happily accepted. We went and sat in the main room with all the pictures and the one of Grandpa on the mantel, which ignited the conversation once again. "So dear …" Grandma began, "… you were going to tell me how you knew my husband." She finished, glancing over at the picture with very loving eyes.

"Well, Grandma Angel," I started, looking over at Cody for an indication of how I should continue. He just smiled and nodded his head as if to say "Go ahead, she'll understand." So I did, "He was very close to the ocean as you know. I used to watch him fish these waters. Grandpa Angel would fish with such respect for all the living creatures, he would only take what he knew he could sell, and he only took what he intended to sell, and no more. He also did something ...," I took a deep breathe as a tear ran down my cheek. "It might sound funny to you, but after a day on the water fishing, before returning to you here, he would always give thanks to the ocean for it's bounty. He took time to appreciate the gift that it had given him." I smiled as another tear fell off my cheek. Cody reached over and took my hand in his.

"He was a great man." Cody said softly. "He died when I was 7 but I still remember him and his love for our family and the ocean." Cody finished, very lovingly giving my hand a squeeze as he mentioned the ocean.

Grandma looked at me carefully when she asked, "But my dear, how could you have known him so well? You would have been so young to have figured all that out, and I don't ever remember hearing him talk about you."

I couldn't help but smile, "Oh he spoke of me often. You just didn't know it was ME he was speaking of. Remember when he would come home and say to you, *'Oh Pearl was in a fine mood today. She was calm and our bounty was good Victoria, really good.'* Or he might say, *'Victoria, something has got my Pearl real stirred up today.'* "

Grandma sat for a minute as though listening to a voice from another time. Cody and I just waited for her to speak next. Grandma's face was relaxed, yet it showed no indication of how she was going to react, though my words were surely running over and over in her mind. Finally, her eyes glanced to Cody, but came to rest on me.

My eyes were on her and my hand still in Cody's, when Grandma's mouth finally opened to speak. "Why are you here, dear? surely, you haven't come just to date my grandson. No offence Cody. I understand that he is a very good looking boy, but if what you say is true, then why? Why here? Why now? And why Cody?"

As I looked into her eyes I could see she really was quick, and understanding; after all, I really hadn't given her much to go on. "Well..." I began, "I need help, and I can't get it from just being in the water anymore. People don't see me anymore. They don't respect the water and what it has to share. They seem to fail to see that before you can take, you must give, that way Thanks can be given both ways, and life can remain in balance. The scales of balance have tipped so far that my ocean is now in real jeopardy, and we are not sure if they are tipped too far for the wrongs to be made right in time. Grandma Angel, your husband Frank understood me in a way that most young fishermen fail to see, or grasp, or care about. Frank understood the balance, and because of that I always felt there was hope...hope that things could right themselves. Do you remember, two days before he died, he asked you to take him to the water's edge?"

I waited for Grandma to answer. She opened her mouth, but moments passed before any words came out. "Yes, I remember..." she began slowly, "he hadn't spoken for weeks and his face was so frowned I worried that he was in pain. All he said was, 'Pearl', and I knew I had to get him down to the water. I called Paul on the telephone, and he came right away. We had all been waiting for something. Everyone's concern had grown for Frank so much; we knew it had to come to a head at some point. When he asked to go to the water's edge, we all knew he was starting his good-byes."

"Well, that day that you and Paul brought him down to me," I began, "he had been considering what would happen to me in the future. All those days he had been sitting, wondering, and worrying, while his health continued to fail. The longer he sat, the stronger his awareness of my realm came into focus for him. Frank was beginning the change." I laughed under my breath, "Or as you call it, he was dieing. He had always lived his life so close to me, that my world was the first to have meaning for him. He started to confuse the two realms. He was speaking to me, but he hadn't completed the change yet. I had told him there was nothing he could do anymore for me as Frank Angel. He had loved me all he could, and yet there comes a point when one can't fight for what is right anymore. The body wears thin and tired, and must look for help. Which is exactly what Frank ended up getting…and giving." As I spoke both Grandma and Cody's focus were unwavering; neither of them moved an inch. "When Paul and you brought Frank down to me, he was close, but still wasn't sure he could do more in the other realm. Do you remember the eagle?" I stopped and looked into Grandma's eyes as she searched her memory.

Slowly her mouth opened, "Yes, it was so beautiful. We took Frank down to the chair on the point." Her thin finger stretched out from her hand and pointed to a single heavy wooden chair perched right beside my ocean. "I put cushions on the chair and a woolen blanket. I couldn't bear the thought of him catching a chill, he seemed so frail."

Grandma stopped speaking, but the look on her face told me that the image of her husband that day was still so vivid in her head.

I continued to recount the day, "Once you and Paul had Frank in the chair and comfortable, he asked you to leave him for a time." Grandma's eyes were glistening with tears. "After you and Paul walked up to the house, the eagle came and sat on the arm of Frank's chair." Grandma's head nodded slowly as she remembered watching from the place where we now sat. "That eagle is a very special friend of mine. He has helped our kind for some time." I continued, "He spent time comforting Frank, assuring him that the fight was not over yet, and that if Frank wanted, he could continue it in the next realm. However it would be in a much different way, more different than anything that he was familiar with.

Frank's love for me and all that I embodied, was what drove him to want to help so much. And I am so thankful for that." My voice cracked and I stopped for a minute, letting my words settle in with Grandma and Cody.

I put my hand on Grandma's hand and looked deeply into her eyes. "Do you remember standing here with Paul, watching the giant eagle take flight from Frank's chair?"

"Yes" Grandma began, "we saw it before, but didn't know it had come to rest anywhere near Frank. Naturally, we wanted to make sure everything was okay, so Paul and I hurried back down to his side." Grandma's voice slowed, "Once we got down to him, I was so surprised. That look of worry, the intense frown, were all but gone from his face. He had this look of peace. It was right then when I had a pang in my chest, and I knew without a doubt that his end was near. I remember Frank looking up where I stood and saying '**Victoria, it's all going to be fine. Pearl is going to have more help now**'. I didn't understand what he meant, but it seemed to bring him such comfort that I didn't ask questions." A smile broke over her mouth, pushing up her cheeks that were now sodden with tears.

I continued to recount the day, for it was a very important day to me too. "You and Paul took Frank back up to the house. His health declined at an alarming rate over the next couple of hours. I waited by your point until finally Frank could join me. We soared together through my waters. I felt a mixed sense of emotion from him as we visited places I know he had only dreamed of. After he had enjoyed the ocean, he prepared for the next leg of his journey, but before he continued, he asked one small favor of me. As I will always feel indebted to him for all of his help from past and yet to come, I was only too willing. Frank asked that I give you this," and as I took my hand from Grandma's, I opened her fingers with mine, and there in the palm of her hand sat one perfect pearl.

Grandma's eyes flicked from the pearl, to me, and back again. Her eyes finally settled on the pearl, and she ran her finger over its smooth white surface. "It's so beautiful...do you ever *see* him, dear?"

I smiled, "Not in the way you mean, but sort of, and you would be foolish not to think that he visits your point every chance he gets. His love runs very deep for you Grandma," I placed my hand back on top of hers, that now squeezed the pearl tight. "Remember. He is only a thought away; as quick as you can think of him, he is back by your side. His love runs deep inside of you and always will."

Grandma looked comforted by my words. Nevertheless, her eyes looked heavy. I realized the night grew thin. With all of our chatter, the hours had just slipped away. Any doubt that Grandma may have had in the beginning of our chat seemed to be gone, and the pearl remained tight in her fist now. We all sat quietly for a moment; Grandma and Cody had a lot to digest from the evening's conversation.

I waited for any further questions, but none came. Cody reached over and took my hand in his, while Grandma just seemed to be lost in thought. "Are you okay Grandma?" Cody asked breaking the stillness.

"Oh yes dear, better than you could imagine. However, I fear the night has slipped away from us, and I do feel quiet tired. I don't mean to be rude, but perhaps I should retire for the night," Grandma said trying to contain a yawn.

"Of course Grandma, Naida and I can clean up. You go on to bed and we will let ourselves out when we're done. I have my key and can lock the door when we go."

"Oh Cody that would be lovely." Grandma turned slowly towards me and drew in a deep breath. She opened both her arms and I accepted her embrace warmly. "You have given me so much tonight dear, thank you" she breathed.

"Sleep well," I said, "and dream of Frank. I would think you would enjoy being with each other tonight". I smiled and we released from our hug. Grandma had a rather sleepy smile on her face.

"Yes, that would be nice." Grandma turned and hugged Cody. She whispered something softly in his ear and released him. Moments later we heard the stairs creak and knew that Grandma was making her way to her bedroom.

"You okay Gills?" Cody said as he slipped his arms around my waist. I stood at the kitchen sink cleaning up our plates from the evening. Cody kissed me gently on the neck and reached for one of Grandma's lacy tea towels to dry the clean dishes with.

"Yeah, I just didn't remember that Frank was your Grandfather until tonight. After I saw his picture on the mantel, so many pieces fell into place. Frank used to bring you to the ocean when you were little, when you used to see me in the water. Now I remember seeing the two of you together, it wasn't just you and your Dad, you would come with Frank too. Sometimes Grandma would come, but most of the time it was just the two of you. Wow! The connection is so clear, I can't believe I'm only seeing the entire circle now." Though I was speaking to Cody, I was also saying it to myself.

CHAPTER 18

Rejected

We finished cleaning up and made our way back outside to Cody's car. Once Cody started the car, we gave it a minute to warm up, and while we did, Cody reached over and took my hand in his. "You know most girls wouldn't like going to my grandma's house for a date, but somehow I thought you might like it better than a restaurant, bar or movies. Was I right?" he asked.

"Oh yes, tonight was wonderful. And your grandma is just as amazing as Frank used to tell me she was," I said.

"Grandpa used to talk to you about Grandma?" Cody said questioning me.

"Oh yes, all the time. When he was out fishing he would talk about all sorts of things, and though sometimes I couldn't stay and listen, more often than not I could and did. He loves your Grandma so much," but before I could continue my body gave a light shudder.

"What was that Gills, you cold?" Cody asked, concerned.

"No, but I do think my body is telling me it's time to store up some more energy. We should get back to the cottage. I need to tell Mother about tonight ..." but just then my body shuddered again, and a look of worry come over Cody's face as he put the car in drive and we sped away from Grandma Angel's warm home on the point.

I didn't feel very strong at all so when Cody reached over to take my hand in his; I just put my head back in the seat and allowed my body to relax. Before I knew it we were back to the spot on the street from which I knew my ocean was just over the hill. Cody threw the car into Park, and as he did, I reached for the door to open it, but it was alarmingly difficult to lift my arm up to the handle, or for that matter to lift my head off the back of the seat. It was frightening just how drained I had become from the night. I couldn't remember ever feeling this bad before.

Just then Cody pulled open the door and waited for me to climb out. It was a good thing he was standing there, because as soon as I tried to push myself out of the seat and get to my feet, my legs gave way and I would have hit the ground if Cody hadn't caught me.

"Hey Gills, come on. Anna is going to think you've been into the wine." He gave a little chuckle, though concern was on every inch of his face. Cody looped his right arm under the bend in my knees while his left arm was gently but securely around my back. I just let my head lean into his chest while he shut the car door with his foot and made his way down to the ocean.

Mother and Chief Greyfeather must have been outside when Cody crested the hill because, though I couldn't see them, I could hear them at Cody's side. "What's happened Cody, why is she like this?" Mother asked quickly.

"I was going to ask you the same thing. One minute we are chatting with my Grandmother and cleaning up from dinner, and then before I could get her home, she's like this. I've never seen her lose her energy so quickly before," Cody said.

"Okay well, get her in the water and instinct will take over, she'll know what to do," Chief Greyfeather said reassuringly.

I could feel Cody's steps quicken, and soon I could hear Cody splashing into the water. I felt the water hit my foot, then my leg and bum. Cody went deeper, but we only got wetter, and my body remained human. There was a surge of pain that shot through my body like a bullet, but still my body remained the same in its physical state.

I heard Cody cry out, "Why is she not dissolving? She's in deep enough; what's happening?"

I heard Mother in my head, "Naida, you must let go and connect with your source now."

Still in pain, I couldn't use my physical mouth to talk to her so I spoke back in my head, "Help Mother, I'm in pain and can't get away from it. Why doesn't my source want me? Help me,...oh please ..." but even as I spoke through my head to mother, I could feel that connection being cut off, like a tunnel, closing around me and I knew that I had to keep it open, but was unable to find the way to. The pain stopped. It was dark all around me, but more importantly...I couldn't feel Cody anymore.

Where was I, and how could I get back to everything that I loved and needed?

CHAPTER 19

Rally The Team

CODY:

The great eagle circled my head, "Cody get back to shore now. She's not changing and we need you back on land; hurry." But she's got to change, she needs her source, I thought. Reluctantly, I pushed through the water back towards the shore. Naida's body lay limp and lifeless in my arms. As I stepped out onto land, Anna pushed forward and took Naida from my arms.

I heard Anna let out a sigh, "What, what is going on?" I cried, terrified of the answer. Chief Greyfeather and Anna stood looking at each other and then back down at Naida's weak body in Anna's arms. Finally, Anna turned to me and said, "She's not here or there. She is in between; for how long, I'm not sure. But you can be sure that if she moves on into the next realm, life will change in this one." Anna spoke sadly.

Just then the ocean began churning. Within minutes the waves were bigger than I had ever seen them. As the waves crashed, we could barely hear one another speak. Anna beckoned for me to follow her and Chief Greyfeather to the cottage.

Once inside, Anna made her way up the winding stairs where she lay Naida's body on the closest bed. The sound from the ocean was muffled inside the little cottage, but not by much.

Chief Greyfeather turned to me, "Cody you must go and get your father. It is most important we gather anyone that can help." He put one hand on my shoulder, "this is what we have been trying to prepare for, Cody. We must hope that we have laid enough of a foundation upon which to stand." Chief Greyfeather finished.

Anna turned and said, "Go now Cody, the clock is ticking." I took one more look of Naida's lifeless body which lay curled up on the twin bed, like a child having an afternoon nap. I felt my eyes moisten, but knew I had to get moving, so with only one thought of saving Naida in my mind, I hurried down the stairs and out the front door of the cottage, leaving Anna and Chief Greyfeather to watch over my Naida.

I made it to my car in record time. As the sand had done once before, it seemed to churn under my feet, moving me to my destination faster than I could have gotten there on my own. Not stopping to try to process what just happened, I jumped into my car and drove.

It was pretty late, but I figured my Mom and Dad would still be up, likely watching TV in their room. As I blasted through the front door, I was met by Mom just turning to go up to her room. Now in her housecoat and slippers she turned quickly to look at me. "Cody" she yelled "why are your clothes soaked? Go upstairs and change before you catch your death of cold like that." Though she catch me off guard when I first charged in the word *death* snapped me right back on task. "Not yet" I panted "where is Dad?" "He just left, got a call from work that the tides where exceeding record heights. Dad was to report to the Dalhousie Pier right away." As Mom got the last word out of her mouth I was reaching for the door to go after him, but before I could pull the door far enough open to go through, it was shoved closed again. Mom was a lot stronger than she looked. "No way mister", she said, "you go and get those wet clothes off right now". But before I could argue, she was pushing me up the stairs to my room. I was pretty wet and thought instead of yelling, which would waste more time; I did as she insisted.

After a very quick change, I pulled open my door to the hall and found Kailey standing there. "What is going on, and can I come, wherever it is you're going?"

"No," I yelled, but just then I felt a tug in my heart and thought "**why not?**" Maybe she could help somehow. "Sorry Kailey, grab your coat and I'll explain everything on the way to get Dad".

Just then we met Mom at the bottom of the stairs, "Where are you two off to at this hour?" Mom asked.

"Mom grab your coat. I need both of your help and I don't have time to stand here to explain…please just come with me."

Mom's face turned to one of worry but she did as I asked. She grabbed her gym bag from the front hall closet and followed us out the door. Mom jumped into my car with Kailey already in the backseat.

As we drove to the pier I explained all about Naida, Mother Terra, Chief Greyfeather and everything else that had happened since I met Naida, up until tonight. They both sat just listening quietly. The odd time Kailey let out a sigh, as if a piece of a puzzle were fitting into memory she had.

Once we reached the pier I told Kailey and Mom to stay put; it would save time. They just sat in the car digesting everything I had told them, while I ran up to where I knew Dad would be stationed. "Dad!" I yelled as I caught sight of him standing with a group of colleagues and students reading over reams of computer paper. He turned his back on the group and made his way over to meet me. "Dad, Mother and Chief Greyfeather need you. They asked me to come and get you," I said, panting as I desperately tried to catch my breath.

"What, now? But ..." Dad said stammering to find the words.

"I know, it's Naida...please Dad, you must just come ...now!" I said trying to find the right words to make him move his feet, but as nothing else came out, it must have been the look on my face that did it. "Mom and Kailey are waiting in the car...please, Dad."

Paul paused for a moment. "One second", he said as he returned to the group of people he had been standing with. I watched him mutter something and take his cell phone out of his pocket. One of the other men took his out too. After the two of them added something to each of their phones, they shook hands and Dad, with a hurried step, made his way back to me.

I started walking to meet his stride and we continued back to my car. I filled him in on the way. Dad, of course had less catching up to do because of his previous meeting with Mother Terra and Chief Greyfeather. Just as we reached my car, Dad's cell phone began to ring. He dug into his pocket and took the phone out.

A look of surprise came over his face when he read who the caller was. I heard him on the phone "Mom, are you okay?" he paused for a moment and continued, "Yes, well now is not a good time." Again he waited for the caller to reply, "Okay Mom, calm down, just sit tight and we'll come get you."

He closed his phone and looked at me, "We need to get your Grandmother, but your car won't hold everyone. Drop me off at my car in the employee's lot and I will run over and get her. We will meet at Naida's cottage."

Dad pulled open the car door. Mom was changed into her workout clothes from her gym bag. Dad lifted an eyebrow at her, obviously questioning her attire. Mom just said, "Well, I couldn't go running around Lunenburg in my housecoat now could I?"

I quickly drove over to Dad's car and jumped out with him. "Dad, you take my car over to the beach now. I'll go and get Grandma. Mother and the Chief need *you* now."

"Okay son, but be warned. Your grandmother sounded really upset."

I jumped into Dad's car and he went one way, and I the other. Soon I was back at Grandma's house where she sat perched in the window with her coat and purse in hand. Seconds later the door swung open and out flew Grandma, pulling the door shut and locking it in one swift movement. If I didn't know better, Grandma was moving with the speed and agility of a 20 year old. Before I could get the car door open for her, she was yelling at me to get back in the driver's seat and sit down. She plunked herself in the front seat and pulled on her seatbelt, yelling, "Drive kiddo." She shot me a wink and I did just that.

"Grandma what has gotten into you?"

"Cody, I will only need to explain it again when we get there, so if you don't mind, I'd like to do it only once." Grandma finished with a soft smile.

"Okay" I said. I got us back to the beach cottage as fast as I could. As soon as our feet hit the sand, it happened again, confirming what I thought I had felt before. The grains of sand moved us at an alarming speed down to the cottage.

A big smile came over Grandma's tiny face but all she said was, "WOW". I smiled back and pushed open the cottage door. There inside sat everyone, including Naida's two sisters, Aella and Fina. Mom was involved in what looked like a heavy conversation with Anna Terra, and Dad sat with Chief Greyfeather. However, once we entered the room, all conversation seemed to finish, and all eyes came to rest on Grandma.

"Hello everyone, this is my Grandmother Victoria Angel. Grandma this is …"

But before I could finish, Grandma put her hand on my shoulder and said, "Thank you Cody. I had the privilege tonight while you were getting your father."

She smiled and took a seat near Kailey. "You see dear, Chief Greyfeather, Anna Terra, Fina, Aella and the others came after your Grandpa Frank and Naida left."

My jaw dropped, "Naida?".

Grandma continued, "Yes, though she wasn't like Frank in that she couldn't speak, and she wasn't as …" Grandma paused looking for the words, "clear…MMM, visible."

My face immediately turned to Anna Terra to translate the meaning of what Grandma had just explained. "It's okay Cody, she is still in between, but like I said before, we are not sure for how long," Anna Terra said to reassure me. Anna now turned to Grandma: "Please tell us all that was said when you saw Frank."

Grandma cleared her throat and began, "Well I had done as Naida said. When I left she and Cody earlier tonight, I went up to my room and closed my eyes in my bed. It wasn't hard to dream of Frank. He was everywhere in my head, almost like he wanted to get in. So before I knew it, there we were, sitting on our point. He gave me a kiss and asked how I liked the pearl." Grandma looked at everyone in the room and then said,

"Naida gave me a pearl earlier tonight. She said it was from Frank," Grandma paused and smiled. She opened the palm of her hand to reveal the perfect pearl for all to see.

Anna Terra smiled and said gently, "Carry on Grandma".

So Grandma did, "Frank said that he and others like him had been visiting all the fishermen that fish these waters every time they slept. They were all communicating the same thing; *take what you need and no more, give thanks for your bounty and no amount of money is worth the harm you're causing.* He said that tonight they will repeat the dream over again to each fisherman, but tonight they will also show them a pearl, like this one." Grandma held up her hand that was closed around the pearl. "In the morning each fisherman will wake with a pearl tucked tightly in the palm of his right hand. They will not be able to take to their fishing boats in the morning...the water will be far too rough. That is when Naida came, she stood behind my Frank and smiled at me. Oh Cody, she has such a lovely smile. As I watched Naida and waited for her to become clear, she just shook her head, and opened her hand to show what looked like a pearl. It was hard to see, though, not like Frank's at all. Frank told me, that Naida had been forced out of her water tonight. Every time the fishermen fish and disobey nature's laws of balance, they put negative energy into the water. It was able to get strong enough tonight to overpower Naida when she tried to connect. Now with her *in between* she cannot control how angry the water gets. Frank said the water will not settle until the laws of balance are put right. And that's where we come in. Each day until we are successful, we will call for a meeting with the Fishermen's Alliance Group. And believe me they will only listen once their wallets start to hurt. So it shouldn't take too long for some. Once they are ready to listen, we will need to explain all of this. Frank told me we would have some more help at that point, but for now we must just ask for the meetings and wait."

I felt my heart quicken and a bead of sweat form on my brow. Apparently, my change also caught the attention of Anna Terra and my own Mom. Mom spoke first: "Cody, it doesn't sound like there is much else we can do. I know what you're thinking, but you must be strong and positive for Naida's sake."

I made a long slow blink with my eyelids and Anna Terra spoke. "Cody, we need you to keep watch over Naida and alert us to any changes in her. Are you strong enough to do that for us?" She looked very seriously at me.

I nodded my head, and before taking to my own post, everyone was assigned a job to do.

Anna Terra, with Chief Greyfeather at her side said, "Paul, Kailey and Emily, you talk to anyone that will listen about this. We need as many supporters as possible when we get to the meeting. Paul, you need to call the Alliance every day until they are ready to listen. Aella, you keep watch on the water; without Naida it could be quite mean. Fina, first of all, you stay out of trouble. I really haven't got time to be cleaning up any messes, and you've got to realize by now that if this is the end of Naida. Yours may not be too far off."

Fina had a shameful look come across her face as she said, "I will try to keep watch on some of the fishermen here in Lunenburg, encourage the meeting, and such." Mother smiled, "Just stay out of trouble. Grandma Victoria, you have the biggest job of all. When we get to that meeting, you will be speaker, and don't forget you will have help at that point. Keep that pearl close to your heart."

Grandma smiled and accepted her task without a second thought. Anna Terra continued, "Now everyone, please get some rest or join your source. Tomorrow is going to be tiresome for all of us."

As everyone got up to do as Anna Terra asked, my father came over to me and put his hand on my shoulder, and said, "We'll do all we can to get the meeting in place quickly. Do you need anything?"

I smiled at my dad; he was so caring and had always supported me throughout my life. "No Thanks Dad, I'll be okay for awhile."

Aella said good night to everyone and walked out the front door. I knew it wouldn't take her long to join her source. Meanwhile, Serafina lit a fire in the cottage fireplace and waited for it to build, and the others to leave. Grandma went home with Mom, Dad and Kailey, but before they left, Mom came over and said, "I will be back in the morning with food and some fresh clothes for you. It sounds like it could be a couple days before things start moving, so I'll make sure I bring enough." She gave me a hug and followed Kailey out the door.

Grandma hung back just long enough to shoot me a wink and say, "Grandpa is doing all he can, Cody. You must believe in him; he won't let us down." She smiled a very proud smile, believing in her heart that as long as her husband was on the job, everything would be fine. Dad took her arm and together they left the little cottage. As I turned my back to go up the stairs I sensed that Fina couldn't wait any longer. I heard a light *whoof,* and knew she was with her source now too. I didn't wait to see what happened to Anna Terra and Chief Greyfeather. I wanted to take my place beside the woman I loved. Even if she didn't know I was there.

CHAPTER 20

The Wait

As I got to the top step I let my eyes fall onto the first bed closest to the stairs. Anna must have changed her clothes because the others would have been wet from the ocean water. She lay on her back now, with warm sweat pants and a sweat top on. The top was one I had seen her wear before; it was her U. of Dalhousie one.

I sat on the edge of the bed just looking at her. She looked so peaceful and calm while her waters raged just outside. I bent down to kiss her forehead and realized she was a lot cooler than normal. I reached over to double check the temperature of her hands, and they too were a lot cooler than normal. There were warm blankets under her, which I left and grabbed blankets from the next bed beside her. I tucked her in, to try and keep what heat she had left close to her body. She still felt cold, so I decided to slide under the blankets with her. I spooned in behind her tiny body pressing as much of my body around hers to keep her warm. It seemed to help, but I'm not sure who it helped more, her or me.

What seemed to be moments later, though it couldn't have been, because the sun was already up, I heard a load crash outside the cottage. I slid out of the bed and pressed my hand to Naida's cheek; *much warmer*,

I noted in my head. Then I hurried to the tiny window that looked out onto the ocean; the waves were crashing, and I wondered just how much longer we would be safe this close to the ocean.

I heard the call of a gentle familiar voice, "Cody, are you up dear?" It was Mom. "I've got coffee and breakfast, among other things."

By the time I got down to the kitchen, Mom had set my breakfast at the table and was putting the other things away in the cupboards. She said,"This stuff should tide you over for awhile. Oh, and the bag on the couch has some fresh clothes, your toothbrush, and other stuff I thought you might need."

I leaned over and kissed my Mom on the forehead. "You eat and relax a bit dear. If you don't mind, I would like to go up and see Naida," she asked.

I nodded my head approvingly and smiled a half hearted smile. "She was so cold last night Mom, I ..." but as I searched for the words, Mom just reached out and gave me a hug. "Things will work out, Cody. They just have to."

Mom stayed for only a short while. After she left, I returned to Naida. I decided to read to her 'cause I didn't know what else to do. It passed the time, but not very quickly, so I decided to find the little TV Anna Terra had bought to entertain me the last time I was left to wait and worry over Naida. I remember thinking then that when I got her back I would never let her go, and look at us now.

Setting it up in the bedroom, I was able to get one channel. The local news report was on, and it was all about the ocean. "Raging storm keeps all fishermen off the ocean for the day. Financial analysts estimate millions will be lost if it lasts the week." Perfect, I thought to myself. Let it hurt your wallets, and make it quick.

10 fishermen had already lost their lives trying to brave the waters. The reporter had speculated that those fishermen were likely pressured so hard from the companies that funded their boats, that they felt they had no choice but to try. So far, every one that had tried, had in fact failed.

Everyone would come and go from the little cottage, except for me. They would bring me news that wasn't being reported on the TV, food, and reading material.

Aella had watched helplessly as each of the now dead fishermen set out to try to fish their waters. She would recount their struggle and inevitable fatality to whomever was with me at the cottage upon her return. Poor Aella would just sit and sob as she tried to wipe the images from her mind.

As far as I could tell, Fina was keeping to her promise to Anna Terra to stay out of trouble and help out. She was regularly reporting back with news of the fishermen and the talk amongst them. The deaths of the others had shaken them, and they were quickly learning that no one was safe out there on the water.

My Mom, Dad and Kailey had all been quite successful in gathering interest and support in our favor. According to Kailey, most everyone she had spoken with felt sick over the current state of the fishing industry. Kailey was creating a blog on the internet; the group that followed it grew daily.

I continued to keep watch over Naida and she continued to fail. Her body grew colder each day. On the forth day I met Anna Terra in kitchen while I was getting an apple Mom had brought for me.

"Cody," Anna Terra said, "How are you holding up?"

"I don't know how much longer she can keep hanging on," I said, looking at Anna through heavily-watered eyes.

"I didn't ask about Naida, I asked about you?" Anna said very firmly.

"I'm okay, I guess. I feel like she is slipping away and no matter how tightly I try to hold her, she just moves further..." my frustration and fear shook my voice.

"Cody, you should know that Chief Greyfeather has been checking on her. Though, he can't hear her, she is becoming clearer in the other realm. He has been noticing though, that when you are next to her, she is pulled back closer to this realm. It is important that you stay with her as you have been doing. Cody," Anna Terra paused taking a deep breath. "It won't be long now. I have called everyone together tonight, here at the cottage. Cody...the alliance has called a meeting for tomorrow...they are willing to listen. I only hope they hear us."

I felt my knees weaken, as I threw my arms around Anna for a quick thankful hug, and ran back upstairs in silence.

When I got to the top of the stairs I noticed Naida looked colder than ever. Her body looked so tiny and frail; her lips had a bluish tinge to them. Quickly I wrapped her in the blanket. I curled it around her body and I picked her up in my arms. I sat down on the bed with my back against the wall, and Naida in the blanket in my lap. I bent my head down and nestled my nose into her hair. Breathing in deeply a couple times, I tried to take in all that was left of her. I whispered "Naida, please hang on...I need you. Don't leave me."

As I sat holding her tight, words came into my head that I was sure were not put there by me. *Don't let go of me.*

"Naida" I whispered, but all I heard in return was *Please Cody.* "I won't, I'll be right here waiting for you."

Just then I became aware of a figure at the top of the stairs. "Cody, we are nearing the end of this fight; the next 24 hours are crucial. You hold in your arms the thread that can keep things together, or unwind life as we know it. Hold on tight." Chief Greyfeather laid a feather beside where I sat holding Naida. He brushed his fingers through Naida's hair and placed his hand on my shoulder before returning to the stairs to join Anna Terra. They stood together waiting for the others to arrive.

CHAPTER 21

Meeting

First I heard Aella and Fina. They had likely been the easiest for Anna to have gotten hold of. Next I heard Mom and Kailey come in. Kailey called up a hello to Naida and I. I called back the hello.

A few minutes later, Dad and Grandma joined the group, making the team complete. I heard everyone take a seat in the room just below Naida and I.

Anna cleared her throat and began, "We've got it. The meeting has been set for tomorrow at 9:00 AM at the beach club. It was one of the only facilities big enough to hold everyone. Are all of you ready? There are going to be lots of questions and we need to be prepared."

As they all got down to work, I heard Grandma ask Anna Terra, "How is Naida?"

Anna just replied, "Weak," and though no one asked anymore, they all knew they would only have one chance to save her. I could hear the keys of Kailey's laptop clicking as she frantically updated her blog and the other communication sites she was using to rally people with. Anna Terra

TIDES

and Chief Greyfeather worked with Grandma preparing her for what she needed to present. I didn't hear Aella or Fina anymore, so I just assumed they had left on other tasks.

Mom and Dad came up the stairs. Mom reached the top first, "Oh honey" she said as she rushed to our side. She bent low over Naida and kissed her forehead. Mom lingered there for a moment and then I realized she was checking to see whether Naida was still breathing. Before she stood back up, she pressed her cheek against mine, "Oh Cody dear, be strong. We are almost at the end." Mom turned her face and kissed my cheek.

Dad just smiled and said, "We are proud of you son, and no matter what happens tomorrow, know that you are never alone. Our love lives in your heart and all that you love. Know that we will do all that we can to win this, not just for Naida, but for life as we know it."

It was just then that the beautiful grey coloured feather that the Chief had laid next to me began to shake slightly, and a small light came from its shaft. I turned to get a better look at it and confirm what I thought I had just seen. It was still as it had been when the Chief put it there. I looked back to Mom and Dad, and they just smiled, not seeming to have noticed anything at all.

"Thank you guys ..." my voice cracked a bit. "You've been so understanding, helpful and supportive. I don't think I could have asked for two better parents."

A tear ran down Mom's cheek as she cupped her hands around Naida's face and kissed her once more. Now looking up at me, the tears flowed freely down her face. She kissed me and ruffled my hair. Turning, she touched Dad's hand and said, "I'll meet you downstairs."

Dad just smiled and raised his eyebrows at me, "Well ..." he said, "we are going to prepare for tomorrow now. Do you need anything...food?"

"No, I'm really not hungry …" I said, as my voice seemed to trail off weakly.

"Okay. Well make sure you let someone downstairs know if that changes," said Dad as he smiled and touched his hand to Naida's cheek. Stopping at her chin, he gently lifted her head slightly. Gazing at her face he said, "We are all working together, really hard, so you hang on in there, okay."

I heard the whispers of Mom, Dad, Anna Terra and Chief Greyfeather just before the door opened and closed again. It sounded as though Mom and Dad had left, and Grandma stayed with Chief Greyfeather and Anna Terra.

My arms start to get numb from being stuck in one position for so long. Never the less, that didn't seem to matter in the least to me. Naida's lips were still bluish, but I kept her wrapped, and as warm as I possibly could. I felt my head nod forward a couple of times, but I never loosened my hold around Naida.

Then the sun seemed to bring new energy into the room. A beautiful stream of morning sunshine shone through the tiny window of the cottage that faced the raging ocean.

I heard a tiny rustle at my left side and realized Grandma had made her way up to us. "Good Morning Cody', Grandma said softly.

"Is it, Grandma? Is it a good morning? I hope so," I said with a heaviness in my voice.

"Oh most definitely Cody, because today is the day Naida will come back to you," Grandma smiled, her cheeks pushing her glasses up her nose.

I hadn't thought of it that way before and as I did I couldn't help the tears. They began to soak my face.

"Oh now, now Cody, do you doubt this old woman?" Grandma asked. I shook my head, and she continued, "We will get through to everyone and all will be put right. You know that in your heart, right? Anna Terra and Chief Greyfeather along with many others," Grandma said, with a very proud look in her eyes. "They are all helping me in my task, and Victoria will be victorious today." She smiled with no hint of doubt or question on her face.

"Alright Grandma…Thank you. I love you," I said with a half hearted smile. Grandma kissed Naida and I, and returned downstairs.

Another visitor entered: Chief Greyfeather. "Cody, do see this feather?" He said picking up the feather that he had left on the bed the night before. I nodded my head yes. "When we are all away at the meeting, you and Naida will stay here at the cottage. If for any reason you feel like you're losing Naida, like she is slipping away, take this feather…but you have to be sure you're losing her. It will keep her tied to you.

My eyes brightened, "For how long? Why haven't I done this sooner?"

The Chief's face went very serious. "Cody, this bind can be fatal, so you must be sure, and you both can't last for long in that state. So be sure."

"I got it, I got it, be sure." I said looking at the feather more carefully.

"Just place it between you so you can be heart to heart with nothing but the feather between your hearts and flesh," Chief Greyfeather said. He stood very straight, and then turned to go back downstairs.

Before his foot could touch the first step, I asked one more question. "Chief…have you seen Naida…I mean…well you know …" my voice trailed off 'cause the truth was, I wasn't sure I knew what was I asking.

He turned slowly, meeting my eyes with a very deep intensity, "Yes, I check on her often." A smile of compassion came across his face. "She is stronger, and has hope when she feels you close. The way you have chosen to hold her …" The Chief chuckled slightly, "I know it reminds her of when the two of you spent some time at the ocean. Remember, you didn't like the feeling of her slipping away, and she learned how to stay in your arms and not join her source. Well, she is using that memory to keep herself grounded to you. Because this time it's not her source that is the other draw, but that would mean something much different for all of us. Thank goodness your draw is equally as strong." The Chief ended with another smile.

I gave Naida a gentle squeeze and nuzzled my nose into the top of her head. Chief Greyfeather knew I was finished asking questions, and made his way down the stairs.

I whispered into the top of Naida's head, "If you can hear me, please Naida, hang on. I'm not letting go without a major fight so please …" Naida's body gave a light shutter and relaxed into mine again.

Anna Terra called up to me, "Cody, you should eat something before we go, dear. It could be a long day here on your own." Before I could answer I heard her on the stairs. Seconds later she stood beside the bed with a plate full of food in one hand, and a glass of milk in the other. "Would you like me to hold her while you take a very quick break?" Anna asked very softly, as if she didn't want Naida to hear.

"Do you think I can? I mean I would like to use the washroom more than eat, really."

A smile broke across Anna's face, "Yes. Of course dear, I will hold her like you and I will yell if anything changes, just don't be too long. We don't want to push our luck."

I stood up still holding Naida, but as I did so, I wobbled slightly, forgetting just how long I had been sitting with her on my lap. My legs felt numb so I handed Naida over to Anna. A blast of cold hit my chest where Naida had been leaning against it.

Anna just smiled and all she said was, "Hurry!" So without a word I bolted down the stairs to the bathroom, catching a quick glimpse of the ocean in its full rage.

I was only gone a minute or two but Anna had a look of worry on her face when I returned. "It's certainly not me she wants." A smile turned up one corner of her otherwise concerned mouth. Anna uttered a low sigh as she handed Naida back into my arms and I could feel a comfort come back into her body.

Naida knew it was my arms that were back holding her, without a doubt. "I think I will wait awhile before I eat. Do you mind leaving it on the nightstand?" I asked. "Thank you so much Anna."

Anna Terra's face was very serious, "You keep a close eye on her while we are gone please, Cody. I can't bear the thought of what life would be without her; I'm sure you can't either. You know what to do if you feel her slipping away?"

"About that Anna, how will I know for sure that it is the time…I mean, I understand what Chief Greyfeather wants me to do. I get that part, but how will I be sure?"

Anna Terra's face softened and a smile of understanding came over her face. She replied, "Oh Cody, do you know that feeling of warmth that you got in your chest when you first met Naida? The warmth that has been there ever since?" She placed a hand on my chest beside were Naida's head lay. "It's not like a temperature kind of warmth it's …," but before she could finish, my head started nodding with understanding,

"Okay I get it. If that feeling starts to grow cold, then I use the feather."

"Yes that's right Cody…flesh on flesh, heart on heart."

Anna made her way back downstairs. I heard Chief Greyfeather say, "It's time to go. We'll meet the others at the Beach Club. Are you ready Victoria?"

My Grandmother's voice sounded strong and confident, "Yes,…Frank and I are ready." I knew as long as she felt Frank was by her side, she could do anything.

I yelled down to the group, "Good Luck; we will wait for good news." I tried to sound cheery.

Grandma called back up, "Thank you Cody, we'll see you and Naida soon."

I heard the door shut and knew it was just Naida and I left in the cottage. As I sat quietly, I could hear the crashing sounds of the ocean, and hoped it wouldn't be too long before the ocean was calm again. I nuzzled my nose into Naida's hair and placed my lips on her head. I kissed her and said, "Hang on, it won't be long now. I know it will all work out." I put my head back against the wall and let out a sigh, and thought, *Please Please Please, I'm not ready to let her go. Please make them listen.*

I took a couple bites of the sandwich Anna Terra had left for me, and put my head back against the wall.

Though I didn't have a clock, it felt like hours went by with no word. I had nothing to do but wait, and as I did so, at some point I drifted off to sleep. In my dream I was standing in water with my Grandpa Frank by my side. Grandpa Frank said to me, "She's beautiful, isn't she? You have a very special bond with her." As Grandpa smiled at me, I could see Naida standing behind him; though she was not as clear as Grandpa, she was truly beautiful. My chest felt so hot; my heart beat so strongly at the sight of her. She smiled, but said nothing. As I watched her, she grew clearer and clearer. And though I could see her clearer now, there was something inside of me that grew; a sadness that was filling the spot where the heat had been so intense. Just then Grandpa, who I had almost forgotten, yet was still standing there said, "Cody, Cody you must wake up now. Please." But I didn't want to. Naida was becoming so clear; why should I wake up from this dream? She looked so beautiful. Grandpa stepped into my line of vision, "Cody this isn't just any dream, **please, please find the feather.**"

Then I understood why she was becoming so clear. As I forced my eyes to open I became aware of the coolness within my chest. "NO, NO, NO, NOT NOW NAIDA, THEY'RE NOT BACK YET. PLEASE, NOT NOW."

But it was now, she leaving and I didn't have much time. I reached for the feather, and it wasn't on the bed anymore. "No! Come on. Where is it?" I said to myself. I placed Naida down. I jumped up from the bed. Hastily, I got down on all fours and clawed at the floor; it had to be here. It couldn't have gone far. I spun around; I caught sight of it.

The feather had fallen under the nightstand. I grabbed it from underneath the stand. It glowed a brilliant white at the touch of my hand. It seemed to know it was needed.

As I got to my feet with the glowing feather in one hand, my eyes fell onto Naida's body. The expression on her face was now one of pain. That was definitely a change; her face was always peaceful since she had been in this state, even when Anna Terra held her earlier. Though Naida's body had tensed, then, her face didn't look like this.

Chief Greyfeather's instructions were at the ready in my mind: *between the hearts…flesh to flesh.* Quickly, I tore off my shirt, being careful not to drop the feather. Though I had no idea what to expect, there was no hesitation in my actions. Without thinking I removed Naida's sweat top. I lay down on the bed beside her, and rolled Naida on top of me. Without a thought of doubt, I slid the feather between our naked chests.

Blackness then…Naida, I could see her, and she was smiling back at me. "Cody, you're here but …Oh" Naida had a look of realization.

"Wait a minute, I can hear you Naida. I couldn't before; what's happened?"

Naida let out a sigh, and as soon as I thought about hugging her she was in my arms. A smile broke over her lips. "Oh Cody, you had to use the feather didn't you? I could feel myself leaving but I couldn't stop it. The feather has bound me to you." Naida finished with a gentle smile across her face.

But I, still not completely understanding, said, "… but I thought we were already bound. I thought we had already established that months ago."

"We are, but now so are our bodies. They will stay that way until your body, can no long support both of ours, or the binding is broken. Chief Greyfeather is the only one that can break the bind. The feather has alerted him to the fact that you had to use it, so he will be aware of the fact that they are truly on the clock now."

Before I could say anything, Naida took my hand and I could see the room now. Though it was blurry I could make out the four beds and the top of the staircase. On top of the bed closest to the staircase was what appeared to be a bright white cocoon; it shone so brightly, that it was painful to really look at. The harder I looked, the more I understood what I was looking at.

It was our bodies, and the feather had created a cocoon around them both. Though the cocoon was opaque, you could make out my body on the bottom and Naida's on top, though if I didn't know who it was, I wouldn't have been able to tell.

"So your body is sharing my energy right now?" I questioned Naida again.

"Yup, now aren't you glad you ate a bit of that sandwich Anna brought up to you?" Naida smiled, and though a smile was on her lips there was much sadness behind it.

"So what happens now?" I asked, hoping she would fill me in on everything else she knew.

"All we can do from here is wait. We can move from place to place, but we can't be seen, by most anyway, and we can't be heard by anyone."

We sat quite still for a moment, and then it hit me. "We can move, right, and you know how to do that?"

Naida nodded her head slowly and as if reading my mind she said, "We could go and watch the rest of the meeting. Then we would know how it is going, and how much longer it should take."

With the next thought we were there. There were so many others, all blurry, but so many. At the front of the room stood my Grandma Victoria. My grandpa was beside her, though he looked quite wispy compared to her.

As a matter of fact, the room was filled with wispy and solid and it wasn't just people; the solids were, but the wispy were people and ocean creatures alike. The solid people acted as though they couldn't see the others, however Anna Terra, Aella, Chief Greyfeather and Serafina were all aware of everyone in the room, including Naida and I.

Aella came over to us as soon as she saw us. She sighed as she examined our state, "So we're really into the last stage of all of this. The Chief said it had happened, but I had hoped he was mistaken. I should never doubt that man. Are you both okay, I mean are you comfortable?"

Naida nodded her head and Aella understood that we were alright for the time being. A man sitting in front of where we were, turned around to "shhhhh" Aella, but when he recognized it was her standing there, apparently alone, he lifted one eyebrow and narrowed his eyes at her. I guess he thought she was talking to herself. Once he turned back around, she smiled at us and raised her eyebrows. Though Naida and I couldn't speak, we were really good listeners, and it sounded like the meeting wasn't going in our favor at the moment.

A very large man in the front row stood up and said "Now listen here, we agreed to hear what Paul Angel, the Professor at Dalhousie had to say on the matter, not his Mom. No, disrespect intended Madam, but I hardly think you have the information that we need." The chubby man's comment was just what Grandma needed to get going.

Grandma cleared her throat, and as she did, I watched Grandpa put his arm around her. As if she could feel him there beside her, a smile broke over her face and she was filled once more with confidence. "I beg to differ with you sir. I believe I do have the information you require, so I need you to sit back down, and listen up."

The man did so and as he did he reminded me of a little boy having been scolded by his mother. He sheepishly took his seat and didn't say another word.

"My husband fished these waters for many years," continued Grandma, "but over the last couple of decades these waters have been violated in ways unimaginable to most old time fishermen. Many of you have checked your morals at the door and done as you please. Well, let me tell you ..." Grandma paused for a moment and took a deep breath, ""The ocean will have it no more." Roars of laughter and ridicule filled the room, but Grandma just patiently waited. "You find it funny!" she finally said, after the room calmed down, with an emotional quiver in her voice. "Do you find it funny then, that you have lost 10 men, and will continue to lose more until you make some big, but much need changes? Perhaps, when your companies are broke, and you find yourself working at the local Mac's Mart, you won't find it so funny." Grandma stood pointing at three of the men sitting off to the side, who were clearly not trying too draw to much attention to there presences there. But it would seem Grandma Victoria knew who they were.

One of the three men stood up, and stated, "That's not going to happen, madam. The waters will calm down, and we will go right back to fishing as we always have. Now, I think you have taken enough of our time. Please take a seat and let us get down to business." The man finished and looked quite proud of himself for trying to put Grandma in her place, however Grandma looked like she barely heard the man.

"Well, thank you for you comments," she replied, "however, you apparently didn't hear me very well, young man. The ocean has had enough of your unloving money hungry ways, and it will not let you, or any other person working for a company, fish until things are settled. Now I would imagine that quite a few of you are losing your shirts this week, and I can guarantee you that not all of you will ever be able to have the business you once had." Several coughs and shifting of seats could be heard throughout the room. "We, meaning all of you, are taking too much from the ocean too fast, and so much is getting wasted daily. That has to stop. Not all of you need to fish, and not all of you need to take as much as you do. There was a time when people took only what they needed, and gave thanks for what they took. It is important that this practice be restored into the fishing industry." Grandma went on; most listened while some just squirmed in there seats. With the look of doubt still present on many faces, Grandma decided to play her only trump card. She, Anna Terra, Chief Greyfeather and Frank all knew this was it. "All of you have had the same dream for the last month."

The looks of doubt now changed to looks of confusion. "That's right, all of you have had dreams of the ocean and its suffering," Grandma continued. The light of understanding appeared to dawn on many of the faces; most looked distant as if revisiting the dream in their minds. Grandma could see it in their faces too. "Yes, you know what I'm talking about. Your dream gave the ocean a human name…Pearl."

Then Grandma held up between her forefinger and thumb, the pearl Naida had given her. The entire room was silent, even the men who had tried to get Grandma Victoria to step down, looked at Grandma knowingly. "So none of you think this is some kind of joke or trick and yet you understand that my words are true. Open your right hand. For some of you this will be the last gift the ocean will ever give you. Others that are able to make the changes, and fish with respect once more, shall be permitted back in the waters."

Each person in the room opened their right hand to reveal a tiny pearl, similar to the one they had received the morning of their dream. Several people got up and left the room, shaking their heads as they left. Others just sat with looks of confusion on their faces.

Grandma just waited. Finally one man, closer to the back of the room, got to his feet when the room had settled back down. "Victoria is it?" Wanting to make sure he had her name right. After Grandma nodded her head he said, "So what do we do?" Looks of triumph came over Anna Terra and Chief Greyfeather's face.

Just as I was getting ready to hear Grandma's response, a feeling of weightlessness came over me. I turned to look at Naida and the same look of concern was on her face, too. "Naida what's happening?" I asked quickly.

Naida no sooner got the words, "We better get back to our bodies," out of her mouth, when we were already back.

The bodies were still cocooned, but the brightness of the cocoon was very dull compared to what it had been.

Naida said as she turned to look at me, "We won't last much longer like this. We are too weak, and Chief Greyfeather can't possibly make it back in time."

"But Naida, we did it! You heard that man. They want to know how to do it. How to make things better!" I no sooner got the words out of my mouth and my vision went black, and I was floating. I didn't feel scared or sad or anything, but one thing concerned me, yet I could not find my voice to call out.

Where was Naida? I couldn't feel her, and I couldn't feel anything in my chest. I couldn't even tell if I *had* a chest. In my mind I was calling Naida, but no sound would come. Then there was Nothing.

CHAPTER 22

Hoping For A Swim

I couldn't tell you how much time passed, if any at all, but suddenly I was lying face up on the bed, as if feeling my body from the inside for the first time. I was cold, I was hungry,…I was confused. My body ached as though I had just spent the last 5 hours at the gym, with no break or water. Thirsty, yes. I was thirsty, but none of this seemed important 'cause something was missing. Something that was very important was missing now. My eyes flew open when I realized what it was. The weight, that should have been on top of my body, was gone. Naida was gone.

I heard a joyous screech come from someone beside me. It was Kailey, who had apparently keeping watch over me. I wanted to get into a sitting position, but nothing seemed to happen when I told my limbs to move. Kailey could see I was trying to do something, "No way mister, not on my watch," Kailey began in a very military tone. "Anna Terra he's awake," Kailey called out.

"Yes dear, I got that from your happy little squeal a moment ago. I'll be right up with some liquids for him." Anna said.

So many questions ran through my head, but I hadn't the strength to ask them. It was like I was a pea inside a pod; I didn't feel big enough to fill the pod, let alone move the pod or communicate through it. Kailey held my arm; as if by touching me, she was helping me somehow. "Oh Cody, I hope you can hear me. You scared us. I didn't think …" but she stop talking and tears just streamed down her face. Kailey's bottom lip quivered as she tried to choke back the tears.

Then I heard Anna Terra, in a calm reassuring voice behind Kailey say, "Good job, you can let go now…I'll take it from here."

"Are you sure if I take my hand off that he won't…you know…?", Kailey asked questioning Anna for good measure.

Anna smiled, "No dear, as weak as he may be, we've got him back. Now give me some room so we can make him stronger."

With Anna's reassurance Kailey gently, and still a little tentatively, lifted her hand from my arm. I felt a slight wobble in my stomach as she did so, but she didn't seem to pick up on any changes.

Anna whipped into Kailey's spot beside the bed, and moved my cumbersome body into a position better for taking fluids. She put pillow after pillow under my head saying, "Well we've come this far with him, we certainly don't need him choking now." She lifted a clear glass full of a thick green liquid to my mouth. It had a straw sticking out of the top, which she pushed in between my lips. "Cody dear, I can only take it that far. The rest is up to you." Anna prompted me to do the rest.

It took all my strength and concentration to suck the liquid into my mouth, but once it was there, I could feel the energy streaming into my body. I could feel it tingle, as it seemed to rush through my body, waking up all the cells on its way. It felt like it was inflating the small pea inside the pod, and soon the pea would fill all the space within the pod.

I heard Anna say, "Slow down there Cody. I know it feels good, but we need to let your body adjust. Can you speak yet?" she questioned.

As she removed the straw from my mouth I turned all my concentration onto my vocal cords. Hoping they would work for me, I opened my mouth and a crackly squeak came out. Anna smiled then pursed her lips and bobbed her head, "It'll come, and it slowed you down a bit too. Here, try some more."

Placing the straw back to my lips I drank. This time I didn't have to concentrate nearly as hard. I could feel the tingling in my chest now; everything was starting to wake up again, and it felt good.

Anna watched me as I drank, "I bet you have a thousand questions going round and round in that head of yours, and no way to get them out yet." Anna smiled as I continued to drink. "Well, I will answer the only one that really matters, to you anyway."

Anna paused, looking quite pleased with herself for knowing exactly what was going on in my head. "She lives! She is with her source getting strong again, too."

I stopped drinking and let Anna's words sink in, savoring the picture she had just put into my mind. One of Naida…alive! I felt a single tear leave the corner of my eye and trickle down my face.

Anna said, "Hey now, that is valuable salt water, mister. Don't go wasting it in tears. Naida is in a very similar state as you, however, we had to get here back into the ocean to nurture her back to health. Yes, the ocean took her back and there have been many more changes since you would have seen it last. Just wait and see." Anna smiled, and I could feel the corners of my mouth do the same. I couldn't wait to see Naida.

Anna kept up with the green cocktail for what seemed like hours, but I didn't care, 'cause it was working, and Naida was alive. Nothing else seemed to matter now.

TIDES

I must have fallen back to sleep because when I woke, Anna Terra had been replaced by Grandma Victoria. It seemed that my voice was back too. "Grandma" I said still rather weakly.

"Oh yes dear, don't talk. Anna Terra said you should continue to save your energy. Here. She wants you to continue to drink this. I hope it doesn't taste as bad as it looks."

Grandma handed me another tall glass with a straw out the top, which I started sipping on as soon as she handed it to me. "Oh Cody, just wait until you see the changes. You'll be so happy. Frank and Naida are surely pleased. Everything worked out so well," Grandma paused, "well almost everything."

I stopped drinking and raised an eyebrow at Grandma not understanding what she meant. "Oh no dear, please keep drinking. I was just referring to the poor men that didn't stay for the rest of the meeting. The ones that thought I was full of 'you know what', dear." I thought to myself, Grandma never could say a bad word, even if she really wanted to.

She continued as I continued to drink, "After the meeting, a couple of the big wigs thought they would go out on the ships to prove that it was all hog wash and things could continue right on the way they had been going. Well, they didn't get out very far before two of the 3 ships capsized, killing everyone onboard. The third ship just barely made it back in to shore. It didn't take them long to come and find us. They wanted to know what they had to do to be able to fish again. News of their return and change of heart traveled quickly throughout the fishermen and reaffirmed everyone's commitment to the change. Oh Cody, wait 'til you see." Grandma said again with a huge proud smile.

I noticed as Grandma spoke that she wore a new necklace around her neck, with a locket dangling from the end. She caught my gaze on the locket, "Oh do you like it?" she asked. It had the pearl from Naida nestled in the front, and when Grandma opened the locket, a picture of Grandpa Frank stared back out at me.

"It's very beautiful Grandma, very special." I pushed myself up on the bed and was quite surprised at the strength I had gained since I first woke up.

I had one thing, and one thing only, on my mind, and that was to get out of this little cottage and down to the ocean to see Naida. In one fluid motion I swung my legs over the edge of the bed, and before Grandma could tell me not to, I was trying to stand. I no sooner got my to my feet when both of my legs buckled under me, sending me right back on the bed from which I had come.

"Oh dear Cody, please stay in bed. Anna Terra told me you would likely try to get up." Grandma scolded. "She assured me that Naida won't be strong enough to see you for a bit either, so just lie down and build your strength, dear." Grandma added thoughtfully.

Just then Anna Terra appeared at the top of the stairs, with a very concerned look on her face. "Cody, it's important you take this time to strengthen your body. We nearly lost the two of you. It's going to take some time. And like Victoria said, Naida isn't strong enough to see you yet anyway."

"Have you seen her Anna? Is she getting stronger?...Has she...asked about me?" I begged, my voice trailing off at the end.

A smile broke over Anna Terra's face, "Yes, I have seen her. Yes, she's getting stronger and she never stops thinking about you, let alone asking about you."

I felt a pang of excitement at the thought of Naida asking about me, and I couldn't wait to hold her in my arms again. "When will we be able to see each other?" I asked Anna Terra.

But before she could answer Grandma leaned over me, kissed my forehead and said, "Cody dear, I'm going to let you two talk. I'll be downstairs if you need me." Grandma shot me a wink, and a smile to Anna Terra, as she made her way to the staircase.

Anna Terra said, "Cody, as you know, Naida came to land to seek help. To save the ocean from the constant violation her waters were experiencing, she had to make the connection with you. You could say that we are in uncharted waters now. We hadn't planned on what was to become of your relationship that you have so lovingly built."

My body felt numb and I couldn't make any words come to my mouth.

"Cody are you okay? I can't tell what you are thinking," Anna said.

Finally my voice found my mouth again, "I can't live without her." That was all I could find the words for. I needed her in my life, I thought to myself.

"I see that with both, of you and the council is discussing what is to happen next. I just don't know…we have never had a situation like this before. Cody, it's important that you continue to strengthen your body and get back into good health. Please…don't worry. We will figure something out for the two of you. Naida needs it just as much as you," Anna finished with a smile and gave my shoulder a gentle squeeze.

I threw my head back onto the pillow and sighed.

I thought I would shut my eyes for a minute, but when I woke it was nightfall and from over in the corner of the room I heard a familiar voice, "Hey buddy nice of you to wake up," Dad spoke as he stood at the window with his back to the ocean and a look of concern on his face. He came and sat on the bed next to the one I was lying in. "So how are you feeling, ocean saver?" He shot me a wink.

I waited for a minute before answering, assessing every inch of my body and as I did, a loud grumble came from my stomach.

Dad laughed, "Good news, I'll be right back." He seemed to sprint out of the room and was back with a plate of food just before the next big grumble was heard. "Here; sit up and let's get this into you." The plate was heaped with fresh fruit, a sandwich, and some carrots. Dad had also brought a tall glass of milk.

I didn't realize how hungry I was until I bit into the sandwich. I just kept chewing until everything was gone. Dad didn't say a word while I ate, he just watched me eat and it seemed with every bite I took, his look of concern seemed to diminish.

As I took the last bite, he let out a sigh. "Feel better, Dad?" I said as I swallowed.

"Yes, I do, Thank You, and how do you feel Cody?" Dad said with a tiny smile.

"Do you think I can try to get up now?" I asked Dad, hoping he would help me even if he thought it was a bad idea.

"Yeah, I would think you should try. Here. Put your arm around my shoulder and I will steady you." Dad helped me swing my legs over the side. He sat down beside me, and put my arm around his shoulder. Holding on to my hand and wrist with one hand, he wrapped his other arm around my back, and together we stood.

My head spun but I could feel Dad steady us. We just stood for a minute, then as he could feel me get my balance he said, "You okay?"

"Yeah, thanks Dad." I could tell he was tired and could only imagine what the last couple of days had been like for him. Watching me regain my strength, and not being sure if all would work out or not.

"Dad?" I said slowly.

"Yes son, what is it?" he said sounding rather concerned again.

"Can we go downstairs? I really don't think I can lie down again," I said, with a smile and a wink.

"That sounds good to me," Dad said, and he helped me down the stairs.

When I reached the bottom I was surprised to see Mom and Kailey sitting at the tiny kitchen table. Anna Terra had just walked in, and Aella and Fina were sitting over by the unlit fireplace.

"Cody!" Kailey screeched. Everyone had already stop talking and had watched us reach the bottom of the stairs. Dad helped me get over to the chair by the fireplace. I heard Mom say, "Paul, did he eat?"

Dad smiled back at his concerned wife, "Yes, he ate it all."

Mom launched herself towards me, wrapping both arms around my neck to give me one of the warmest hugs. "Oh Cody, I've been so worried." She said, "How do you feel son?"

I let a smile break over my face, and I said with a chuckle "Well if I didn't think you would tell me to wait 20 minutes after eating, I would tell you I'm ready to go for a swim in the ocean."

Mom smiled, knowing how strongly I wanted to see Naida. "Soon Dear, soon," was all she said. Mother Terra cleared her throat and Mom released me from her hug and took a step back.

Anna Terra stood looking down at me in the chair, and said, "So you would like to go swimming, would you?" A smile turned up the corners of her mouth. My eyes brightened at the sound of her words, "Come on." And she helped me up using the same hold Dad had helped me with.

I felt a flutter in my stomach; the excitement seemed to fill every inch of my body. Then I stopped. "Wait Anna, is Naida strong enough?" I asked tentatively.

Anna Terra's smile got bigger, "You be the judge." She pushed open the door, and there stood Naida waiting for me.